The Empty Tower

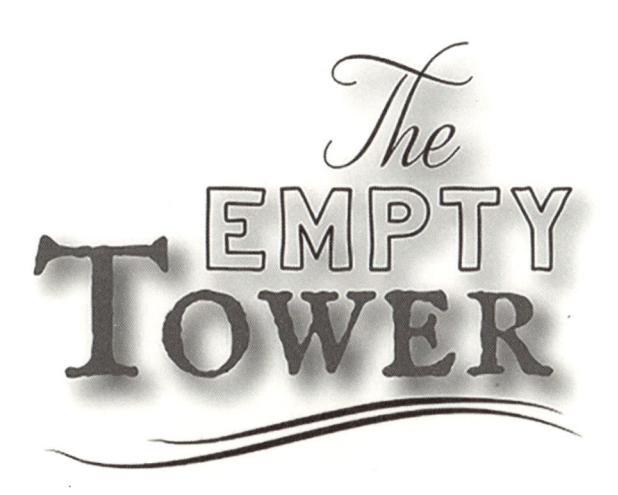

By Jean Bothwell

Cover design by Tina DeKam
Illustrated by Margaret Ayer
Cover illustration by Alex Cherkasoff and Margaret Ayer
This unabridged version has updated grammar and spelling.
First published in 1948
© 2019 Jenny Phillips
www.thegoodandthebeautiful.com

For

EBK

My sister

and best friend

Characters

Premi—A school girl at Charity Abide

Bittu—Another school girl, from the hills

Motibai—Housekeeper for Bittu and her father

Missa*—Miss Margaret Stanton, Principal of Charity Abide School

Dr. Jamna Das—The school physician

Chaman—The garden boy

Teacher-ji—The teacher of second class

Mamma-ji—The school matron

Kamla, Lila, and Tara—Other school children

Khansama-ji—The doctor's cook

---

*This is a title (a contraction of the formal "Miss Sahib") and pronounced "Mis-sah," the two syllables equally accented.

If any character's name proves to be that of a real person, the use here is purely coincidental.

Table of Contents

1. October Morning 1
2. A Lamp for the Goddess 10
3. The Return of Bittu 17
4. Motibai Changes Her Mind 23
5. The Plan. 29
6. Weekend Visit. 39
7. More Grown-Up Advice 51
8. Saturday in the Yard 59
9. Kamla's Question 68
10. Morning of the Fair 76
11. Afternoon of the Fair. 91
12. In the Tower 100

Glossary. 108

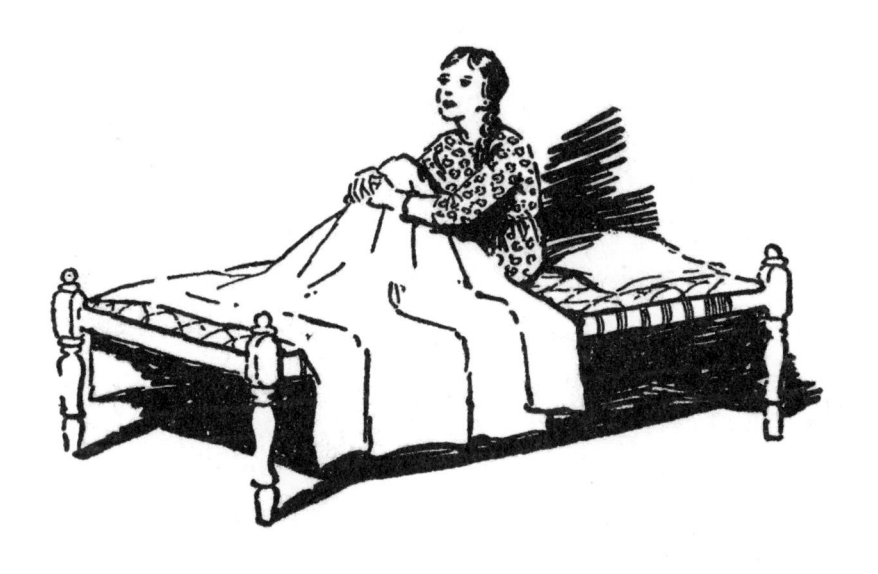

1
October Morning

The long North India rainy season was over. Dawns were clear and bright. The ground was beginning to dry on top and crack a little. There was a different feeling in the air that had been hot and damp all summer. The children could play running games again. They even needed a bit of thin covering at night.

Premi Singh sat in the middle of her bed one morning in early October, watching day come to the school called Charity Abide.

Light had already broken in the east and was shining beyond the trees and over the yard wall when she awoke. The sky was pink through the branches, and there were puffy little white clouds with gold tips at the edge of the pink part. Higher, above the trees, it was blue like the frocks Miss Stanton Miss Sahib wore. Not that anyone ever used that long title when speaking of the principal. It was much easier to say Missa very fast, and everybody knew whom it meant.

All about Premi, the school still slept in its rows of beds set on the verandas of the three buildings that formed the sides of the dormitory yard. Beyond the low roof of the kitchen, which made the fourth side, with the matron's room and the storerooms, Premi could see the red tile of the principal's house where Missa lived and had the school office.

At the right, over the roof of the big girls' dormitory, were the yellow plaster walls and tower of the schoolhouse.

The whole place was so quiet that the voices from the kitchen could be heard all the way across the great open square where games went on after school. The cooks, and the big girls whose turn had come to bake the breakfast bread, had begun their work. Their words ran together and made a low, continuing sound, rising once in a while when somebody laughed.

One bed in the second class row on the veranda of Middle House was empty this morning. It was next to Premi's and belonged to Bittu Kundan Lal, who had gone away in September to stay a while at her father's house in the hills. She was the only hill girl in school this year. Everyone else came from families of the plains.

Beyond Bittu's bed Kamla lay in hers, one arm thrown over her eyes. On the other side Lila too was still asleep. Both would miss the beginning of this beautiful day. If Lila had been awake, she would certainly ask, "What makes it beautiful? How can you tell?"

Premi smiled and lay down again to consider the question without being asked. The answer was all around her. There was the color in the sky, for one thing, her favorite pink.

And there was hunger, though Lila would look doubtful and frown if Premi counted that. But it was a good feeling to be hungry, if one knew that hunger was to be satisfied with warm rounds of bread when the gong sounded. Another half hour must pass before that happened. Then, in the same way that a red clay water jar fell in bits when it was struck with something hard, the quietness would break. There would be nothing but pieces of stillness left between the hammerings of the gong.

Something to look at and something to feel. But there was more, Premi thought. Being at Charity Abide was all of it, really, for Premi herself at least. She repeated a verse in a low whisper:

"May Trust and Truth and Charity
Abide within these gates.
If each who comes
Bring even one of these,
All good shall be
And happiness and peace."

The man who had originally owned the school place had had those words carved on his gate post. How had he thought of such perfect ones? Missa said they had been in his heart first.

"If each who comes." What did the children bring to Charity Abide? The big girls had won a cup for playing basketball. It stood in the assembly hall in the schoolhouse, on a tall teakwood pedestal. It was not a very large cup, but they had won it a second time and a third, so now they could keep it always. Playing basketball for the school was wonderful. But what did the younger girls bring? Nothing. And there wasn't anything they could *do*, either.

Premi wished again that there was something real she could have a part in for Charity Abide. She had talked it over many times with Kamla and Lila and the others in second class. It was too long to wait to grow up and play basketball. She wanted to do something now. But the talking usually ended with Kamla's deciding words.

"We don't have to do anything, Premi," she had said once. "Missa doesn't want us to. She wants us to enjoy school. That's enough for now. But just wait until I get big. I'll be a teacher then, and I'll come back here and look after all of you for her. That'll be my something for Charity Abide."

"But Kamla," they told her, "we'll be big then, too," and Kamla didn't like it at first when they laughed. Then she too saw how funny it was and joined in, until they forgot what they had been talking about. Most of them did. Premi learned not to mention her greatest desire every time she thought of it.

She thought of it now while the light grew and the time for the gong came nearer. Perhaps doing something for Missa herself could mean it was done for the school as well. There were so many things Missa did not have that Premi felt she needed, or the school did. It was difficult sometimes to separate those needs.

There was a motor car for one thing. Though other people had them, Missa went about in an old open carriage hitched to a fat, sleepy white horse and driven by a shabby coachman.

And though there was a tower on the schoolhouse, there was no bell to hang in it. Perhaps the motor car was not important to Missa, but Premi knew that she did want a bell. She had said it more than once.

Premi sighed. How could little girls help with such big things? Most of the children came from homes like her own, in small villages. The fathers worked in the fields to raise wheat and cotton and vegetables. Sometimes the mothers worked with them, and older boys and girls, if there were any. Not all children were sent to school. Her own father worked very hard, but much depended on the harvest. There was usually enough money for the plain, straight frocks that she and Shanti, her elder sister, wore and for their white cotton head scarfs. But not for shoes or school fees. Premi did not mind that so much. Few of the children had shoes and many did not pay. But perhaps if everybody helped... if all the fathers and mothers knew...

She did not finish that thought. She would talk it over with Bittu when she came. There would be a great deal to tell Bittu. She had missed her very much. She had known Lila and Kamla longer, but her feeling for Bittu was different, though Bittu was ten, a year older than she, and a hill girl.

The school cat had had new kittens. Mamma-ji had said Middle House could have one to call their own when it got big enough. Missa's birthday had been last week. Premi had saved some of the sweets, but they would be too hard if Bittu did not come soon. Dr. Jamna Das had made everybody be vaccinated. Missa had been done first, to show the smallest children that it would not hurt. Premi made a face, remembering. Her own had hurt a little. It would take much talking to tell Bittu everything.

Premi lifted her sheet, letting a lot of air blow in under it with the morning breeze, so that it puffed up like a tent. Then she let it fall again with a little snap, and the sheet lay limp above her slender body. The movement sent the heavy gold bracelet on her arm sliding up and down, and she stopped playing with the sheet to admire it.

Because it was the only one she owned, there was no tinkling sound of metal chiming against other metal. But she did not care. She would not mind if she never had another bracelet. This lovely thing was better than having many plain glass ones or even three slender silver bangles, and it held a big place in her heart.

There had been a pair of the bracelets, carved alike in the beautiful three-petaled lily pattern, that had belonged first to Bittu's mother. Then they had been left for the little girl, and Bittu had given Premi one of them before going to the hills for her visit home. It had not been off Premi's arm since, not even for washing.

Premi traced the carving with her finger now, in and out of the delicate flower petals.

She could hear Bittu's words as clearly as if they were only just now being spoken. "Hold out your hand, Premi," Bittu had said, and she had slid the cool, smooth gold over Premi's folded-in thumb and onto her wrist. "Now we are Bracelet-Bound," Bittu had added. "Whatever one asks of the other, that will she do, because we are friends." Premi repeated that too, softly, though she need not be so quiet now. Here and there, heads were popping up from other beds, and little rustlings and sighs meant the whole place would be ready for the rising gong.

Premi leaned over and touched Lila gently under her ear. "Wake up, Lila. It's morning," she said. It had been the same every day since the little girls now in second class had begun school together. Lila always had to be called.

Lila rolled over and sat up, yawning. But the sound of her waking was lost in the larger one. The noise of a hundred chattering girls swelled above the treetops and startled the roosting crows there. They flew off, cawing loudly, black shadows against the bright sky.

When the three friends joined the pushing crowd around the taps on the edge of the big brick washing terrace, near the kitchen, Premi was still thoughtful. She looked about her. This, too, made the day beautiful, though how it was hard to explain. Much yellow and pink soap, having a strong odor of herbs, was being worked into thick white lather on the girls' faces. Some of the fluffy stuff caught in glossy dark hair and shone there for a moment like a wreath of colored bubbles before clear water dissolved it. More fell away in great blobs on the drain water. But it left each face shining and smooth and the skin soft as velvet.

As fast as one girl finished, another took her place. It was a mad, scrambling dash every morning to be clean and have one's plate washed before the breakfast gong sounded. But Premi loved it, and somehow she always managed it with Lila on one side and Kamla on the other, and there would be Bittu, on her return.

When the monitor banged the gong again, they were ready, each with her plate in front of her on the ground. Mamma-ji, the matron, took her place, and the chattering tongues quieted. The baking squad brought out the big baskets of bread covered with squares of white cloth, bumping them along over the uneven bricks in the kitchen veranda floor. Then there was a small, complete stillness. Each child bowed her head and folded her hands and someone started the words of a blessing, set to an old tune:

> *Ai Bap, Tu Roti De*
> *Mujhko, Kuda*
> (O Father, give me bread)

The clear, high-pitched thread of song rose above the morning quietness, floated up and over the wall, and Missa heard where she sat alone at her own early meal. She smiled. Another day had begun at Charity Abide.

2

A Lamp for the Goddess

In the middle of that month of renewal and refreshing after the long rains, came the festival of *Diwali* to celebrate the coming of Lakshmi, the Great Mother, from her summer absence in the hills. Many believed she blessed the new season and made the fields fruitful.

All the people, wherever they were, took part in the festival. There was much work to do in preparation, but afterward there was also much joy when the work was done. For some it meant clean houses, fresh whitewash on the walls, and new hard clay floors. For a few there were new clothes, feasting, and visits.

The children everywhere looked forward to *Diwali* all year long. To them, it meant sweets and holiday and the illuminations on the great night of the festival. Then all the people who could afford it set small oil lamps, *chiraghs*, in rows round the tops of their houses and on the window ledges and balcony railings. And on the last night of the feast they were lighted, at dusk when the sun had quite gone, to guide the goddess back to the plains.

At the most, the children at Charity Abide had expected the usual *Diwali* sweets, made of spun sugar and tinted with lovely color—bright pink dogs and yellow camels and lions. There might be a half holiday from school. Just possibly they would get a glimpse of the town fireworks—rockets trailing across the sky in great showers of light—after it was quite dark and almost bedtime.

But the day before the beginning of the festival they had a surprise. They had finished the school song at Assembly and had sat down again, waiting to be dismissed for classes. But Missa did not give the signal at once. Someone saw the large, square, white envelope she held in her hand. Then others saw it, and the whispering stopped and the wriggling feet were held still against the rough matting on the floor.

She waited until the stillness was like something solid one could reach out and touch, and then she held up the envelope and smiled and said, "This is an invitation for all of us, from His Highness, the Rajah of Mura State, to have places on the roof of his town house for the *Diwali* illuminations, three nights from now. I have replied that we would be happy to…"

They did not let her finish. The assembly hall sounded as if a swarm of bees had stopped in flight and decided to settle there. Premi felt a little chill start creeping up her back and she shut her eyes, feeling she could almost see the lights and the crowd now.

Then Missa could be heard above the other confused sounds saying, "Girls, please, there is more." And she was not frowning.

When the place was still again, she said, "It is fortunate that the Rajah has a big house. There are so many of us. We will have the evening meal earlier, and please all be ready so that we will have time to walk there slowly and get in our places before the *chiraghs* are lighted. You will?"

"Oh yes, Missa. Thank you, Missa." It was as if one girl, with a voice of many, had spoken.

ঙ৪০

No one was late or untidy when the time arrived. The fat, sleepy white horse and the old carriage were in the driveway when the line came out. Missa took the smallest children with her in it. And the carpenter and Chaman, the garden boy, were waiting to walk beside the others, out of the compound and along the road.

It was the first time in Premi's memory that the whole school had gone anywhere together. And Bittu was missing it. Would there be any celebration for her in her father's house in the hills? Then she forgot Bittu for a moment because the line was moving and they were out on the main road.

The sun was going down and sometimes they walked through shafts of light, slanting low and full of the dust kicked up by the girls' feet. But they moved steadily on through the light and the dust until the leaders reached a high gate in a yard wall. Inside, a steep stairway in the Rajah's house led to the roof. It was only wide enough for one girl at a time, and half-way up, where the stair was separated into flights by a wide platform, two men stood with piles of *chiraghs*.

Each girl was given one of the little shallow, red clay saucers. And while she held it, one man poured in a small quantity of oil and the other handed her a thin wick of twisted cotton to float in it. All over town for weeks, the potters' wheels had been turning day and night that there might be enough of the little lamps for everyone.

At the top of the steps, a smiling woman of the Rajah's household gave each girl a light for her wick and showed her where to set her lamp on the edge of the low parapet.

The woman wore a sari of sheer pale-blue silk over darker soft silk petticoats of the same tone so that the whole looked like water rippling when she moved. And the scarf end of it was embroidered in a pattern of lotus flowers, which looked as if they had just been lately plucked from a pool and fastened there. No one saw Premi reach out and touch one of those flowers. It was as velvety soft as it looked, like a real one.

Then she set her light down and went to sit with the others on the thick, soft, cotton rugs that had been spread for them on the rooftop. It was a large space. There was enough room for everybody.

Other roofs on left and right were filled with more people, and across the great park, directly opposite the Rajah's house, on a terrace of the old fort, some men were moving about.

"They will send the fireworks from there," said Kamla. "See that frame in the middle? They use that for the rockets, so they will go straight when they are lighted and not hurt anybody."

All the children looked. It was as Kamla had said. They could see the frame and the piles of fireworks.

Premi clasped her hands together and sat quietly. This was what they had been waiting for, for three whole days—the fireworks and these illuminations which they themselves had had a part in arranging here on this wall of the Rajah's house. She had made a wish on her own light about a bell for the tower—that somehow the children could get one for Charity Abide.

Below in the park, the mass of people in their bright holiday clothes looked like a moving garden where the flowers went walking with each other, instead of staying in their own plots, each with its kind. Even the men's turbans, usually white for everyday, were made of many colors tonight. All of the shades of the sunset were there and the paler ones of the dawn.

It was growing darker. Teacher-ji had tried to explain to them the hidden meaning of this lovely Hindu festival. Whether or not a goddess governed the changing of the season, it was still true that Nature followed a clear pattern. The long months of the rains nourished the earth, and it stored up the water to give food to the seeds and roots in it. And then came fire, in the form of the sun's rays, to purify the earth of the vapors and mists. The fire purified the air as well for man to breathe and grow strong in, after the summer damps.

And now this evening's fires were the symbol of the sun, to make the new season fair as well as light for the goddess to return. Teacher-ji had made everything plain. *Lakshmi,* she said, was really Mother Nature and so was a part of God, the one true God of the Christians.

Here and there over the town, lights had begun to wink faintly through the trees. A little breeze blew the line of light around their parapet. They could not see the crowd below now, but it must be thicker because there was more noise.

And then, deep beneath that noise, from far within the bazaar, all the waiting people heard the sound they had been expecting, and a great roar went up. Drums had begun and their slow regular beat and roll, going on and on, was like the thumping in one's chest when the heart was too full of hurt or joy. The drums meant only that the sun had quite gone and now was the real time for lights to shine everywhere and for the fireworks to ascend.

The faint little flickers through the trees became stronger. Buildings that had been in complete shadow appeared again, lighted by a chain of fire that spread from wick to wick, seemingly blown by the evening breeze, but helped by unseen hands, from edge of balcony to neighboring parapet and on beyond to roofs and domes and spires.

While the first rocket tore up and up and sailed across the sky, the drum beats went on and on. And Premi's heart kept time.

The smallest children were asleep before the last of the rockets and Roman candles and sparklers died and left the sky dark. Here and there the wicks in the little clay lamps had burned out too, making gaps in the lines of light along the buildings. But it had been a wonderful festival. One had only to close her eyes tight to see it all again, as Premi did before she went to sleep, back in her bed at Charity Abide.

Would the Great Mother grant all the wishes that had been whispered above those tiny lamps tonight?

3

The Return of Bittu

It was a bright day early in November when Bittu, the absent member of second class, came back to Charity Abide from her home in the hills.

The mid-morning peace of a garden place hung over the lawns and hedges. Inside the schoolhouse it was still chilly. The doors had been opened to let in the sun-warmed air. But the brick floors were cold for the bare feet that shrank away and up, to be tucked under cotton skirts or rubbed occasionally, when hands were not busy with book or slate.

Second class wriggled and twisted, and after a while Teacher-ji laid down her chalk. "Come," she said. "We will go into the garden and study the flowers."

They crossed the driveway to a part of the garden which was near the main road but hidden from it by a bamboo thicket. They could hear *tongas* going by in the road, and the drivers' voices urging the horses on, and people talking. And then one set of harness bells separated from the rest and the sound came nearer. One of the *tongas* was coming in.

The children forgot the flowers and Teacher-ji and stood still to listen and wait for the little cart that presently came in sight round the curve in the driveway. There was a woman in it and a little girl, and several pieces of luggage were piled in the front seat by the driver. The travelers sat with their backs to him so the children saw the driver first. But they knew who had come.

"Bittu!"

Premi called the name so loud that the horse heard above the jingling of his own bells, and he shied away so that the driver had a hard time keeping the *tonga* upright. But he did it and the horse went on, faster than before, until he was pulled back on his haunches in front of Missa's house, with gravel flying from his hoofs in every direction.

The children looked at Teacher-ji when the *tonga* whizzed by and she nodded and said, "Yes, you may go," and they started to run after it. But Premi got there first.

Bittu was smiling at them. She waved and leaped out and Premi caught her and their arms went round each other. They were together again. Bittu hadn't expected to see anybody, she said, except perhaps Missa, until noontime. And there was Missa, coming through the office door, and Bittu started toward her, with half of second class grasping her hands or the end of her head scarf.

From the top step Premi saw Teacher-ji go up to the *tonga* and give a hand to the woman who still sat there, counting out the fare for the driver. Then she stepped down and the man took out a tin trunk, a large roll of bedding, and a small one. There was a wicker basket, too, and a knobby bundle wrapped in cloth and tied by the four corners.

The woman and Teacher-ji came to the veranda together. When Bittu saw them, she pushed the children aside and came down the steps again. She took the hand of the woman and led her to Missa.

"This is Motibai, Missa. She keeps my father's house. She would not let him bring me. She wants to see for herself where I sleep and where I learn."

She was dressed in an old-fashioned way, with a very full skirt of printed cotton which swirled and rippled about her ankles when she moved. There was a heavy band of plain, dark red material, like a wide hem, at the bottom of her skirt. Her jacket fitted her body smoothly. She had no jewelry except a heavy silver necklace which gleamed through the thin, white, cotton head scarf. She drew a blue woolen shawl more closely about her shoulders after she had given Missa her *salaam* of greeting.

Motibai looked round the lawns and the garden and up at the big white pillars of Missa's house. She nodded her head as if she liked what she saw, and she said to Missa, "Come, young lady. Come and show me everything. Then I will go. I am to stay this night at the house of Dr. Jamna Das. He is the friend of Bittu's father. That is arranged. It is said he looks after these when they are sick." She leaned over and touched the cheek of the child nearest. "H'm. You seem healthy enough." She looked at Missa again. "Now I will see and then I will go."

Missa said, "But you will stay long enough to take food with us at noon?"

Motibai's large old face broke up in a smile, her first. "Ah well, perhaps," she said. "I might stay that long. To see what the child eats. Then I will go."

The luggage was still piled in the middle of the driveway, where the *tonga* man had left it. Missa said, "Children, help Bittu take her things in. And tell Mamma-ji, please, that a guest has come."

Missa and Motibai went slowly round the corner of the house together. Motibai was talking again, and they heard Missa laugh.

Teacher-ji went back to the classroom alone. The children began work on the luggage, with Bittu to say how it was to be divided. The smaller roll of bedding was put on Missa's veranda, with the wicker basket, to wait until Motibai should leave.

They were arguing about lifting the larger roll and the trunk when Chaman appeared and said Missa sent him to help. He took a cloth from his shoulder and wound it into a pad which he fixed firmly on top of his cap. Then he stooped and lifted the trunk up slowly, straightening at the same time, until it rested on the pad. Then he reached a hand out groping for an end of the bedding roll. The children decided to take turns, three at a time, tugging at the other end, and the rest followed Chaman and the first three round the house and along the path to the yard gate.

Premi and Bittu walked together. Bittu was carrying the knotted bundle. She held it up. "Smell! In this I have brought apples from the hills." Part of the procession stopped to take big sniffs. "My father had me bring them. They are from his trees."

Even through the papers inside the cloth, it was a good smell. They stopped at the gate to change helpers, and the bundle went from hand to hand on the way across the yard, for smelling. Some of the children had never seen an apple.

On the veranda of Middle House, the trunk and roll were carefully set down. Bittu looked around. "Everything is just the same," she said.

"It wouldn't change much in two months," said Kamla. "Did you think it could be different so soon?"

"I don't know what I thought," said Bittu, "but it is nice to be here now."

Bittu set the apples on her bed. "We will have these after school," she said. "I want to find Missa and Motibai now. You will like Motibai as I do. She has always been there, in my father's house. She cooks our food and she sews my clothes." Bittu held out her hand. "Now come, let us go find them, Missa and Motibai."

She had pushed up her sleeves and they saw that she wore only one bracelet, the twin of Premi's.

Kamla said, "Have you two marked those bracelets? So each will know her own?"

"Mine needs no mark. I wear it always," said Premi.

"And I," said Bittu.

"But they might come off some time," Kamla insisted.

"But how, unless I myself took it off?" said Premi. She doubled up her fist. "See? If anyone else tried to take it off my arm, I would do this. And if I wish to take it off, it will not slip over my hand until I do this." She drew in her thumb flat against her palm, as she had done when Bittu had first slipped the golden circle over her hand.

"That is right," said Bittu. "For me, too. Don't worry, Kamla."

4

Motibai Changes Her Mind

Motibai and Missa were standing by the front door of the schoolhouse. Motibai was carrying her shawl and she looked warm. They had seen all the classrooms, she told Bittu. She had made her mark on the blackboard with a piece of chalk. "Now I have been to school," she said. She laughed and lifted her hand with a bit of chalk dust still showing.

The big girls had sung the school song for her, and the little ones had given her two of the clay elephants they had been doing for handwork. She brought one out of her pocket for them all to see.

The little figure was the color of modeling clay, dark gray, but the child who made it had painted a yellow blanket on its back and there were red lines across the forehead. It looked like some of the big ones they saw occasionally when a string from the Rajah's table went plodding by on the main road.

"Do you make these, too?" asked Motibai.

Second class answered, together, "Nay, nay, those the babies make."

Motibai's face was solemn. She looked at Missa. She pursed her lips and said gravely, "I see. It is with the mind this second class works. Not any more with the hands."

She did not laugh until Missa did. And then she thrust the little elephant back into her pocket. Because the skirt was so full, the pocket did not show, and Premi wondered how deep it was and what else she carried there.

The gong sounded in the dormitory yard. Somebody was hammering away at the great copper disk under the kitchen tree. It was noon and time for food. The children started down the steps with Missa and Motibai in the middle, when Motibai stopped again. She turned to Missa. "That I have not seen. Where does it go?" She nodded toward a smaller door set in the plaster wall near the main entrance to the schoolhouse.

"That is the way to the tower," said Missa. "There are steps inside so that one may climb. We meant to have a bell up there when the schoolhouse was built, but we hadn't enough money. We will have it someday. It will come. And when it does, the one who rings the bell will go through that door."

Motibai nodded. She said, "But a gong you have. It calls the children. Why do you want a bell?"

"We would not have it just for ourselves, Motibai. It would be for all of Rajahpur."

"But what have you to do with them?" Motibai seemed to have forgotten about food. The children were hungry and Bittu pulled at her skirts to remind her.

Missa had forgot, too. She said, "The tower is high. So many would hear our bell. They know the words that belong to this place, trust and truth... you've heard them. The bell would say that to everyone. You see, Motibai?"

Motibai said, "I see you doing something for people who do nothing for you. That is not good."

"Good comes of it, Motibai. You will see."

They walked together toward the yard and the children followed, looking at each other wonderingly. This Motibai who seemed so much a part of Bittu's family, though neither servant nor relative, was going to be honored today. Missa would eat with them, too.

Premi took her plate and sat down with the others when the song was done, but she forgot her own hunger. She herself would like to see the place that had been arranged for a bell. She had never climbed those steps behind that little door. They all knew it was there, and its purpose, but she had never thought of looking inside. Now Motibai's question had made her want to, very much.

It would be wonderful to have a real bell. Missa's wish had been there, plainly heard again in her voice. Instead of the copper disk under the kitchen tree, hammered with a mallet by the monitors at getting-up time and for food and school and duties and food again, there would be that other note, clear and high up above the playground and the trees.

But a bell would cost much money. Buying a bell would be something for Missa and the school, too, though she had said "for Rajahpur," not thinking of herself. But where would children get the needed rupees, when Missa could not?

Premi sighed and Kamla gave her a poke. "Eat, Premi. Don't go to sleep." Premi looked at her plate. She hadn't started and the others were finishing.

The food was good. Motibai ate two plates of rice and *dal* gravy and she liked it. "You have this every day?" she asked.

"Yes," they said, "every day."

"And what do you eat for supper?"

"Curry with meat, and curry without meat but made with potatoes, and chopped onion with salt, and *chapatties*..."

Missa laughed. "You'd better stay a little longer, Motibai, and see for yourself. You will be welcome."

Motibai looked at Bittu and all the rest of the second class standing there watching her. And beyond them, the rest of the school watched. She wiped her forehead with the end of her scarf. She got up off the stool they had brought out for her. She smiled. When she did that, her round cheeks broke up into many little creases and puckers. It was the same each time she smiled. Premi had never seen anyone's face fold up in just that way. She wished she would do it again.

Motibai said, "I did not like it that my Bittu would return here. But how could I know it would be like this? Things were not done this way in the old days. Girls did not go to school. It was beyond believing, what Bittu said. But now I have seen."

Bittu put her hands together, palm to palm. She touched the tips of the fingers to her forehead, then held her hands up, still laid together, toward Missa and to Motibai.

"If she could stay just one night—in Middle House with us—she would see all. She could go to see Dr. Jamna Das tomorrow."

"But tomorrow I must go back to the hills. I had planned to take the child back with me, if I could, even though I knew the master would be angry. Now she will stay. She should stay. He was right. This is a good place. But I... I must go."

Missa said, "I could send a note to Dr. Jamna Das. He would understand. You should not make the return journey so quickly. You must rest a little. Stay here today. Visit in the class and sleep in Middle House tonight. The children want you."

"Oh yes, Missa," they said.

So Motibai went to school for an afternoon and at supper said that the curry was better than she had expected.

Because Motibai was there, Bittu and Premi had no moment together that evening. Premi would have to wait a little longer to tell everything that had happened while Bittu had been in the hills.

The waiting did not matter to Premi now. She would have even more time to think about getting the bell. She had finished her thought about it that had begun on the morning in October when she had waked so early. And an idea was slowly growing in her mind. If Bittu would help, Missa might have her wish one day. That had been her own wish, whispered softly above the bright flame of her *Diwali* lamp on the roof of the Rajah's house. It had burned steadily through the evening and was still glowing when the line had started down the narrow stairway to go home. Her purpose was good. Surely it would not fail.

5

The Plan

Early the next morning before time for school, Dr. Jamna Das sent one of his hospital orderlies with his motor car for Motibai. Missa had been right. He had understood that Motibai should rest.

The children were allowed to come out with her, and Chaman carried her things. Missa herself shut the car door when Motibai was seated. Through the open window they heard the old housekeeper say, "It is well. I go now. You have made all things pleasant, all things, for me."

Then the orderly climbed to his place. The motor began to hum. The wheels turned, the car started, and she was gone. The children went back to the dormitory to get ready for school. They had known Motibai only a few hours. But they liked her. And now they would miss her. It was a little as if each had had her own mother there for a little while.

That afternoon they ate the apples Bittu had brought. And when the last bites had slowly disappeared and a hopscotch game began, Premi knew the time had come to tell Bittu about her plan for the bell.

It would not matter that Bittu had not yet heard about the things which had happened in her absence. They were gone and she had had no part in them. The plan was something new that she could help with, if she only would.

So Premi led Bittu to the teakwood tree behind Middle House. There the sounds of the yard were muffled and they could talk until suppertime if none of the others had seen them leave the playground.

They sat down on the long, dry grass there, and it was too quiet, because Premi did not know how to begin. Would Bittu help? Did the bracelet promise mean help with anything, no matter what it was?

Bittu leaned over so she could look up into Premi's face. "What are you thinking about, Premi? Is it something nice? Are you going to tell me?"

Premi laughed and nodded her head. "It's about

The Plan

a present for Missa. I know she wants it. And maybe we can get it for her, if you and the others and all the fathers and mothers help." She turned and clutched Bittu by the shoulders and her smile was gone and the words were anxious ones. "You will help me, Bittu? You did mean it, when you said each would help the other in all things because of our bracelets?"

Bittu held out her hand silently. Premi clasped it and there was the ringing sound of metal meeting as the two heavy gold bands slid down their arms and touched at the wrists. "This is the ancient Law," said Bittu. "A pledge like that once given cannot be gainsaid. I will help you. What is it Missa wants?"

The plan became even clearer in Premi's mind as she unfolded it to Bittu, step by step as it had grown from the first. Her own desire to bring something to Charity Abide, Bittu already knew. Now she added her belief that the fathers and mothers would help if they were shown a way to do it.

And there was Missa's own thought, about a bell for the schoolhouse tower, which all had heard. She had spoken of it again on the day that Motibai had brought Bittu back to school.

"But a bell big enough to hang in the tower would cost a great deal, Premi," said Bittu solemnly. "I think so... much money."

"There is a way we could earn it," said Premi. "That is the plan." Her eyes seemed to grow bigger, and they shone with her pleasure. "We can have a fair, like a village market day, and sell things... and we'd invite all the fathers and mothers..."

"But what would we sell?"

"People take things to market in the village here on the plains, Bittu. We'd ask them to bring gifts to our fair and we'd sell what they bring."

"And who will buy?"

"The other people who come... the people of the town... the fathers and mothers of the day scholars... everybody."

Bittu seemed doubtful still. "We can't do it by ourselves, Premi."

"Nay, but all the school will want to help when they know."

"What if Missa says we may not do it?"

"But it's a surprise, Bittu. We cannot ask her."

"'Tis a big plan. I wish we could talk to Motibai. No word has come from her. I thought she would send her *salaams* before she went back to the hills."

"She will return someday. She liked Charity Abide. That I could see," said Premi. "And we liked her."

Bittu stood up. "Come. There is still time before supper. Let us go and look at the place where a bell is needed. That is a good beginning. For then none can argue. We can say we have seen it."

No one paid any attention to them when they walked across the playground, out of the yard gate, and across to the schoolhouse by the usual path. They followed it every morning. But this was Friday afternoon and they were doing as they pleased.

The Plan

The little door to the tower was not locked. They pushed and it opened, and they stepped inside. The place was very still. And it was cold. Sounds from the yard were dulled by the thick walls which also shut out the warmth of the sun.

Narrow stairs at the left of the door led steeply

up to a platform where a bell ringer might stand. They climbed there and their feet disturbed dust and they both sneezed. The echo startled them and they jumped, then laughed at their own fright.

Light came in, they saw now, from four small, round windows high up.

A ladder made of short lengths of bamboo, tied crosswise with hemp cord at each joining to two long poles, stood on the platform, leaning against the wall which they faced as they came up the steps. And when they looked up to see where it led, or why it was there, they saw above them in the shadows, but below the roof of the tower, heavy crossbeams forming the square framework that Missa had said was there. Those great timbers were not a part of the building itself. They were extra and for a definite purpose—to support a bell.

"Missa must have wanted a bell very much," said Bittu. "See, everything is here, ready for it. All but the bell itself."

"That I have already told you, and you have also heard," said Premi. "But now you have seen."

They went back down the stairs and out into the sunlight again, blinking a little. Bittu said, "We should tell the others, tonight, I think, after supper, when the big girls have gone to study."

So, Premi thought, Bittu liked the plan. She had said she would help because of her promise. But she would help more now and work harder because

The Plan

she had seen the proof that Missa really wanted a bell for the school. Now the tower was only a great empty place without sound. But if everybody helped to make their fair successful, it would be filled with ringing.

The word was passed quietly to second class while they were eating supper. Premi and Bittu had something to say as soon as plates could be washed.

In Middle House two beds were dragged close together. The tufted quilts were brought from others and the children wrapped themselves like mummies and huddled in a circle, listening to the plan for a fair, told much as Bittu had heard it that afternoon.

They all wanted to help and they asked many questions. There was a warm argument about the best time to have it, until Premi said, "Christmas is giving time. It is also a spending time of year. It is then we should have our fair. And on the Saturday when our holiday begins will be best of all."

It would indeed. There could be no better time. So that was decided.

And then someone said, "How can we write this to our fathers and mothers? Missa or Teacher-ji will see all the postcards that go out, as they see the ones that come in."

That problem was met, too. They could call on the informal telegraph of India, spoken word from mouth to mouth, that had been effective long before writing was invented. It would be even more effective now. They could tell the milkman and he would pass the message along wherever he carried milk and it would go on from those places, they knew, in the same fashion.

The day scholars must invite their families. All the workmen about the place could tell theirs. And always, to whomever the message was given, must be added the warning that Missa should not be told. For her it was to be a great surprise, both the fair and the purpose for holding it. And things to be sold must be enough to bring in the needed amount for the bell.

"How much will that be?" asked Lila.

That was something still to be found out.

"What will we give for selling?" said Kamla bluntly, when it began to seem as if the discussion were finished.

Premi said, "It is we who are making the plan."

But Kamla was not satisfied. "That's nothing," she said. "And we will be laughed at if no one else gives us anything. You needn't have a fair at all if you and Bittu gave your bracelets. They'd buy a bell. Motibai said they were worth a great deal."

All the children said, in shocked voices, "Kamla!"

But Kamla was not ashamed. She said, "Suppose nobody does bring us anything. And the people will come to buy and there will be nothing for them. Have you thought of that?"

Some of the children said she was right. They

The Plan

talked about what they could do, and somebody felt around in the dark for a stub of pencil under a pillow and another child brought a bit of paper torn from the flyleaf of a little book. Lila crawled out of her quilt and brought the night lantern in from the veranda, and they made a careful list of things they could offer for the fair.

There were flower garlands. Chaman would give them the blossoms they would need from the cutting garden. But they couldn't make those until the very morning of the fair. The babies might be persuaded to make pinwheels and windmills mounted on the small bamboo sticks. And there were kites. If anybody had pocket money to contribute to buy the necessary thin, bright paper, they themselves could make a few kites.

Premi put the list in her jacket pocket. It seemed very short. But at least the fair was started, and she could scarcely wait to hear the new bell ring. That they would be able to have it she did not doubt. People would surely help when they understood.

But Premi found, when the plan was explained to the other classes, that not all the school was as thoroughly convinced as she that a fair would amount to anything. Even her own sister Shanti was skeptical.

"What will you have to sell?" Shanti asked. The other big girls agreed with her when she added, "People haven't things to give. There isn't enough in our whole village put together to help much. What does our father have? Look at our own old jackets! How can you go ahead with this when your own village will have no part? Unless, of course, the head man does something. And who will ask him?"

But even that did not quite discourage Premi. Second class had taken firm hold of the idea, and they held frequent meetings. Their combined hope was enough for the whole school.

6

Weekend Visit

Bittu had not long to wait for news of Motibai. Dr. Jamna Das sent a note to Missa and she called Bittu in to the office to talk about it. Bittu took Premi with her.

It was a lovely day, the kind to make bad news easier to bear and pleasant news more enjoyable. Chaman was trimming uneven places in the lawn. They could hear the click of his shears after they had gone inside the office.

Missa held up an open letter and smiled and said, "You'll never guess what I have here."

She could not see that their hands, hidden by the long scarf ends, loosed their tight clasp. They did not have to guess that it was something good. They could tell that from Missa's voice.

"Motibai has changed her mind again. She has not gone back to the hills. She is not going until the warm weather. It is written here by Dr. Jamna Das."

There was a little silence. Premi pressed Bittu's hand. "Say something," she meant.

Bittu said slowly, "But Missa, what will Motibai do?"

Missa laughed. She said, "Motibai thinks Dr. Jamna Das' house needs seeing to. He has no wife, only servants to look after him. And she likes it here in Rajahpur."

"But Missa," said Bittu again, not needing any prompting now from Premi, "what will my father do? Does he know this? Who will see to our house if Motibai stays here? Who will cook his food?"

"That is decided too," said Missa, looking at the letter again. "He is closing your house, now that you and Motibai are here. He, also, is coming to the plains for the cold weather."

But Bittu was not pleased. She tightened her hold on Premi's hand again, and Premi wondered why.

Missa said, "Here's one more thing. I almost forgot it. How could I?" She read to them slowly the very words of the letter. "With your permission may Bittu come here for the weekend to see Motibai, and bring her friend Premi with her? It will be nice having them."

Weekend Visit 41

Still Bittu did not smile, though Premi could scarcely believe Missa had read correctly. She had never seen the inside of any house in Rajahpur but this. And to be a guest for a whole weekend at the Doctor Sahib's!

Bittu was almost crying and she rarely did that. "I don't want to leave this place, Missa. After a while they will say I may as well stay there all the time and be a day scholar. Wait till Motibai finds out we have some of those."

Missa was not disturbed. "One thing at a time, Bittu," she said. "I myself am glad that Motibai will be near. It will be good for Dr. Das to have his house looked after. And you can talk to your father when he comes. He was willing for you to live here at Charity Abide. I think he will see that you stay."

That sounded better, and Bittu's hand lay loose again in Premi's. One visit might be pleasant, after all.

When the time came, Premi had doubts about her clothes. Her jacket looked more and more worn. But Bittu's jacket was not new. Perhaps her own poor garments would not matter much. They would have to do, anyway. They were all she had.

Dr. Jamna Das came himself for the little girls after his day's visits were over on Friday afternoon. Second class followed them from Middle House across the playground as far as the yard gate to see them off.

It seemed odd to Premi to be out in the public

road at evening time. The street lights were not yet turned on, but they could still see in the early dusk. A lone rider was knocking a ball about on the polo field. They passed a bullock cart piled with sacks of grain. The driver was asleep. Some students on bicycles called and waved to Dr. Das.

A little further on, the car turned in a gate and swooped around the half circle of a driveway and in under a high-roofed *porte-cochère* and stopped. Motibai stood at the top of the veranda steps holding out her arms. A houseman came out and took the one small bundle the children had brought.

"Though the house is different, the welcome is the same, my Bittu," said Motibai. And Dr. Jamna Das, following them inside, said, "A double welcome, because our guests are two."

The next morning they went into the doctor's garden with Motibai. There were tall hollyhocks growing against the wall and small, hardy, yellow chrysanthemums grouped in pots around the sundial. There were roses and marigolds.

"Let's make flower ladies," said Premi. Bittu had never made any, but she saw how it was done when Premi did a hollyhock one with frilly skirts and a sweet pea bonnet for the head. They had a whole new row finished when Dr. Das came out hunting the gardener, who was working near the children and not pleased at all at having the flowers picked.

"So you like it here in this place!" The doctor

looked at his watch and sat down on the bench by the sundial.

"Oh yes, Doctor Sahib. We are having fun."

"All the class wanted to come. They looked very sad when we left."

"They did? We can't have anybody sad in this world if we can help it. I have to go see my patients now. But when I come back, we might have to talk about a party. Then those others could come."

"When can we have it?" said Bittu.

"Now that is important," he said. "You came last night. You are here today. You have to go back tomorrow afternoon. Not much time, is there? Only today."

Bittu and Premi nodded, but he did not see. He had turned to Motibai. "If we have a party this afternoon, it will mean some extra work for somebody. So you, Motibai, are the one to say."

Motibai laid down her sewing. She reached into her big pocket. In her hand, when it came out, was a small, worn black purse. She opened it. The children watched her and almost didn't breathe. What had that purse to do with getting a party ready?

"The first thing when one wants a party is to see if there is money enough," said Motibai severely. "This is your housekeeping money, Doctor Sahib. Let us see!" She poked her finger among the coins and took out the folded notes and counted them. She whispered the amount to herself. "There is enough," she said. The purse went back into the pocket. She got up and straightened her skirts. "There will be a party. See that you are here for it."

A party, with all of second class! In this garden. Kamla and Lila could come, and all the others. And Missa. Premi and Bittu followed Motibai to the kitchen to see if they could help make the party. But she said, "No, I do not need you here. This cook will arrange all things."

They reached the front veranda as Dr. Das came out of his office. He had a note in his hand. He saw their solemn faces.

"Wouldn't she let you help?"

"Nay, Doctor-ji."

"Then how would you like to ride with me this morning? I will drop you at the school and you can leave this note. Then I'll come again after one call and you can watch the car for me at others. I have no driver now."

It was odd to be coming back to Charity Abide such a short time after leaving. And to be coming as visitors, bringing an invitation.

Missa's old carriage and the white horse were standing in front of the house. She was probably about to go to the bazaar. They had come at the right time. They waited on the bench in front of the office. The deep notes of someone's organ lesson came from the direction of the schoolhouse. That was the only sound until they heard Missa inside, speaking to the ayah. Then she came out on the veranda and was so surprised to see them that she forgot her *salaam*.

Bittu handed her the note. Missa read it and smiled. "I should have liked knowing about this sooner, but I think we can manage to get ready for a party," she said.

"We didn't know it ourselves, Missa. It just happened all at once, after breakfast."

"That's often the way nicest things come. They do just happen. Please thank Dr. Jamna Das for me. He has written three o'clock. We will be there."

And then she was sitting in the carriage and the old white horse had to lift up his head and take her to the bazaar, and they were left with the ayah to wait for the doctor.

They saw a great deal of Rajahpur that morning, riding through the shady streets where officials lived and through the railway quarters and even out to a little tumble-down place on the edge of the bazaar where a hospital worker was very ill.

It was a busy time of day in the bazaar. Once, when they were slowed up by a tangle of carts ahead, Premi saw toys in a shop opposite and she said, "Look, Bittu! Across there! See those pinwheels? That's the kind the babies will make for us for our fair."

"Fair?" said the doctor. "Is Charity Abide having a fair? I had not heard of it."

"It's a secret, Doctor-ji. You mustn't tell Missa. It's a surprise for her, to buy the bell."

"Bell? What do you mean?"

So they had to tell him everything, the whole plan. He frowned at first until he understood, and then he laughed. "But you children surely know it will take a great many rupees to buy a bell? I did not know Missa wanted one so much. She should have told. There are people in this town who would…"

He did not finish. The carts were clear and he could go on. When they got out of the car at his house at noon, he said, "I've been thinking about your fair. It is a fine idea, if only for pleasure, and I will help, but I think you should tell Missa beforehand. Sometimes people like knowing better than they do the surprise."

They looked at each other. Dr. Jamna Das was going to help. They had not thought of asking him. But he was a friend of the whole school. They might have known he would want to have a part in their fair.

But when Bittu arched her eyebrows in an unspoken question, Premi shook her head decidedly. No, it would spoil the whole plan if they told Missa.

⊂3≥⊃

It seemed a long time before the party could begin. Perhaps Motibai had changed her mind by this time and would let them help with something. They went through the house and out again by the serving-pantry door and down a little path to the cook house. They began to smell the party before they reached the narrow veranda. Bittu said, "M'm! I'm hungry."

There were four people in the kitchen, but Motibai was not there. The cook's wife was helping him, and a young man was rolling out dough on a low pastry board. A little boy they had not seen before was washing raisins. Fat was bubbling and crackling in a shallow iron pan set on a little charcoal brazier near the pastry board. The pan was black from many such heatings. All the holes in the high earthen stove, built against the back wall of the kitchen, were full of fire, and other things were cooking there. The biggest pot must surely have rice in it. Steam was pouring from the lid.

There was nothing to do now but wait. Three o'clock was hours away.

It took Missa's carriage and the old white horse and a hired *tonga* to bring her and the others to the house of Dr. Jamna Das, and they were there only a little late.

Missa collected all the head scarfs so the children could play more comfortably. Motibai had put her sewing away, but she stayed and talked to Missa.

The children played until they were tired out. Then they came back to the sundial and sat on the grass there, and Bittu and Premi showed them how to make flower dolls. Premi had been anxious all afternoon, fearing some child might forget and say something about the fair. It had been all right while they were playing.

Now Missa could hear every word spoken and it

was Lila who blundered. A fine row of dolls grew from the work of their quick fingers and they set them round the rim of the sundial. "We could make these to go in our garland shop for the fair," said Lila happily. All the others screamed her name aloud and Kamla, who was nearest, put her hand on Lila's mouth, but the word had been said.

Missa looked round at the noise but she saw no quarrel, so she only shook her head at them and turned back to Motibai. She had not heard. The secret was safe for a while longer.

Then Motibai got up and said, "Now we will have the eating."

When she returned, the house man was with her, carrying two trays of food, and he went back for more. That cook had kept his word. There were *teconas*, little three-cornered pastries that had been fried in deep fat. They were still warm. Some of them were filled with curry so hot that it took two drinks of sherbet to cool one's mouth. Others had mixed chopped vegetables inside.

One tray had sweetmeats, some partly covered with silver paper which showed they had come from the bazaar. And there were large, sticky, dark-brown *gulab jhamans* made of sour milk curd and coconut.

And there were salty biscuits, very thin, to go with lemon and oil pickles. And a pudding made of rice, colored with saffron and full of raisins.

The trays were beginning to look a little empty

and the shadow across the sundial pointed to evening before Dr. Das came. He was glad they had not waited for him, he said. He had had some extra calls to make.

They gave him a plate with a taste of everything and he sat down on a bench and ate a little to please them. By the time he finished the sun had gone way down in the sky and they had to go home. Missa stood up and Dr. Das set his plate by and said he would take them all home in his motor car.

It seemed very quiet after the car had left. It had been a glorious day and a wonderful party. The cook had made beautiful food. But Bittu and Premi had eaten so many curry puffs and sweets and biscuits that they did not want supper. When they were ready for sleep, Motibai brought glasses of milk and sat with them until every drop was gone.

"Thank you, Motibai. It was a good party."

"It will be like another one when we have our fair," said Bittu.

"What is that?" asked Motibai.

They looked at each other. Bittu said, "You tell."

So Premi told, and while she was talking the cook came to ask Motibai what he should make for breakfast. He waited politely in the doorway for Premi to stop talking, so he heard, too.

Motibai said, as Dr. Das had done, "It is good to please the Miss Sahib, but I think you should tell her. She will like it better."

Premi frowned and the cook came into the room and picked up the empty milk glasses and said, "You liked my food today? All the children liked it, I think. There was not anything left."

"Oh yes, Khansama-ji," they said together, "it was a splendid party."

He shuffled his feet and said, with a quick glance at Motibai, "They always have food at fairs. I could come and cook for you."

"It would be the Dr. Sahib's time that he pays you for, and his sugar and flour," said Motibai.

"But Motibai, hear us," said Bittu. "You do not know that Doctor-ji has said he will help, too. A food shop for our fair would make it like a real village one."

The children could not go to sleep at once after Motibai put out the light. The words that had been said in this one day already made the fair seem a grander thing than they had hoped for. And out of it would come the surprise for Missa. It must be a good surprise. Nothing must spoil it. She should not be told.

7

More Grown-Up Advice

The last Saturday of every month was visiting day at Charity Abide. Parents, aunts, uncles, older brothers and sisters, everybody who possibly could, came on that afternoon to see the children. They always brought something. That was a part of the visit.

The children whose homes were farthest away did not often see their families. And some of the parents did not come at all during the whole ten months of school time.

Premi's village was one of those far away. Her father came twice a year, once to bring them to school when it opened in July, once to take them home in early May when it closed. At those times he borrowed bullocks and a cart from the head man. He had not bullocks of his own.

On that last Saturday of November, Premi was in the crowd at the gate, with the hopeful ones. It was fun to see who would be called out, though knowing herself she would not be. And later there was always a share in the presents the others had received. It was nearly always food of the kind that could be kept a while for hungry times between meals. There were roasted peas, lumps of brown sugar, raisins, and sometimes nuts and big, round salty crackers. None of it lasted very long. There were too many children who would never have anything extra at all if the gifts were not divided.

Today, Premi's name was one of the first to be called. She couldn't believe it. But the monitor's call came again. "Premi… Shanti… your father has come."

Premi hurried back to Middle House to get her head scarf and to find Shanti, who had not come to the gate. Her heart was beating fast and her first thought was about her mother. Perhaps she was not well and their father had come to take them home. That had happened to other girls and they had never returned.

But there was no sign of the borrowed bullock cart and no look of calamity on their father's face when they reached the veranda in front of Missa's office. He was waiting for them there on the bench and he held on his knees a large bundle wrapped in cloth.

They gave him excited *salaams*, and though Premi saw the bundle at once, she pretended politely not to. Instead, she said, "How is our mother? Why has she not come?"

Her father laughed. "She is well, and thinking only of you. That is why I am here. And are you not glad to see me a little though I did not bring her?"

"Of course, Papa-ji," said Shanti. "She did not mean that. Come, let us find a good place on the visitors' lawn. Not many are here yet. It is early."

He followed them through the arbor covered by an ancient climbing rose to the space set apart for visits. There were benches under the shade of tall cork trees. It was a pleasant place for talking, he said, though he had not long to stay. "I have come walking, and your mother could not walk so far. I had to sleep overnight on the way and she does not like that either. I could not ask for the bullocks for an errand such as this."

They found an empty bench in a corner of the hedge, and he sat down between them. He set the bundle on his knees again and began to untie the knots.

"This is not a good coming time," he said, "but your mother was afraid you would be cold. So these are made." He looked at Premi's thin jacket and at Shanti's, shrunken too, and said, "Your mother was right."

Premi wondered what could be in the bundle. She had not expected anything new to wear this season. Yet clothes kept one warm and the bundle was too small to be even one new tufted quilt. And she knew, too, that her father and mother would not give them one alone. So it must be something to wear. But what?

The second knot was untied. The four ends of the cloth fell away. The father lifted a garment and shook out the folds. "Ah! This is the small one," he said. "For you, my daughter," and he handed it to Premi.

It was a new *bundi*, a soft, warm, quilted jacket, made like her little, old, thin one. But there was no other likeness. The outside of the new one was a heavy homespun print, red, with yellow and blue flowers, and the lining was black. The quilting had been done in diamond pattern to hold the thick cotton interlining firm.

Premi slipped it on. The sleeves were long, right down to her wrists, and it buttoned straight up to her chin, warm and snug-fitting round her neck. It was not too big. It was just right, a wonderful jacket.

Her father turned her round so he could see how it looked. "Your mother will like what I shall say," he said. "It is as if you had been there for it to be sewed. The tailor wanted it different but she said no, it must be this way. It should be done as she said."

Shanti and Premi laughed. It would have been fun watching their mother besting that stubborn village tailor. And then they looked at each other and

More Grown-Up Advice

down at the jackets, Shanti in her blue and Premi in the gay print. The quilting was machine stitched, true enough. This was the first time they had ever owned tailored jackets. Where had their father got the money? How had he been able to give them so much?

He saw the questions coming when they turned to him. They did not need to speak the words. He said, "Do not worry, my daughters, they were good rupees that I earned, and the tailor owed me a favor. I made a good bargain. And now you will not be cold. That is well." He smiled and picked up the square of cloth which had covered the coats and protected them from the dust of the journey. "I will go now. Give Missa my *salaams*. I must get back to your mother and the fields."

He was standing up before Premi remembered the fair. They would not need to send him word by any of the milkman's messengers. He was here and he must stay a bit longer and listen. And another thought gave her courage. If things were going well for father, they might be for others in the village, and something would surely be sent for the fair.

She said, "Oh, Papa-ji, stay a little longer. There is one more thing to say."

He sat down again and Shanti frowned and said, "'Tis a silly idea she has, Papa-ji. You should not let her do this thing." But he held up his hand and bade Shanti be silent and said, "Yes, what is it, daughter?"

"It is for Missa, Papa-ji, something we want to

Margaret Ayer.

do. For a long time she has needed a bell in the tower. See, over there? A bell, for ringing, up high. It is not just for her, but for Charity Abide and for the town, she says. If all of us help, we can get it for her." Premi spoke very fast, conscious of Shanti's disapproval.

"It will cost a great deal," her father said, looking across the hedges and measuring with his landsman's eye the size of the tower. "And I have used all my extra rupees for your coats."

"Nay, Papa-ji, it is not for money I ask. We want things, things to sell in our fair that will be like market day in the village. All will have a part. And we will get the bell."

He nodded his head and Shanti frowned more deeply. "A brave plan, my daughter," he said slowly, as if he were thinking as he talked. "I will see what our village can do. We should be proud to help. Our sons and daughters are learning to read here in the town." He stood up again. "A good plan. When will you have your fair?"

"When our holiday begins, on the Saturday."

"Ah, that will not be long. You have not much time."

They walked with him through Missa's yard and out to the gate that opened onto the main road. They had not taken off their new coats. The bright colors shone in the afternoon light and Premi felt as if everybody must be looking, they were so beautiful. She walked as tall as possible to make the coat look even better.

It was more difficult to say goodbye to their father because they hadn't expected to see him at all. And now he was leaving after he had stayed with them such a short time.

They watched him start down the road and saw him slap his pocket and turn round and come back. He said, "A trifle that I almost forgot," and grinned and handed them each a small bag of parched grain and brown sugar.

"Oh, Papa-ji, the coats were enough. Thank you."

He looked them over again, critically, and had Shanti turn about in hers, as Premi had done. He was satisfied. "Your mother will be pleased," he said.

But it was on Premi's shoulder that his hand lay longer and he said, "You do have permission from Missa for this plan of yours?"

Premi wondered why all the grown-ups talked this way. First, Dr. Jamna Das, then Motibai, and now her father. She said, "Nay, Papa-ji. We mean it for a big surprise. You do not tell about gifts before you give them. You have surprised us with these coats. We did not know you were coming."

That made him laugh. But he looked grave again at once and said, "Somehow this surprise for Missa is different. I think you should tell her about it. It will be better."

She did not promise. He had not asked for that. They gave him more *salaams* to be taken to their mother, and again for the coats. This time, though they waited, he did not turn back.

8
Saturday in the Yard

There was one duty for Saturday the year round at Charity Abide that cold or heat or visiting or even the prospect of a fair did not change. Everyone had to wash her hair, and the big girls helped the little ones.

After breakfast on the first Saturday morning of December, Premi sat by the kitchen door waiting for Shanti to come and help her with her hair. It was too long and thick to do it by herself. There wasn't room at the moment on the terrace by the taps for even one more girl. But from this spot she could easily see Shanti coming. And it was fun to watch what was going on. Someone had got soap in her eyes and was yelling for a towel. The monitor came with the pocket money and a crowd collected around her. But that did not disturb Premi. There wouldn't be any for her. Shanti ought to come any minute.

Premi loved getting her hair done. It was a mixture of feeling and sound and smell. The cool water, the tingle of the soap on her scalp, the earth round the terrace damp from the morning-long splashings, crows cawing in the kitchen tree, and the monkeys scrambling over the tiles of the storeroom roof. It was the same every week.

Then there was the drying and brushing out in the sun, until her hair stood away from her head like a fluffy black cloud. The cold feeling came again when Shanti poured some coconut oil in her hand and rubbed it in her scalp, followed by another brushing until every flying hair was smooth, to be bound into two flat, tight braids.

This morning there was continuous passage in and out of the yard gate. Missa went back and forth several times. Some of the big girls were going to the bazaar with her today.

The milkman came swinging in, and the girls who had crowded round the gate scattered to give him plenty of room to walk. He had a wooden yoke over his shoulders, and he was bowed a little with the weight he carried. Suspended by stout strings from either end of the yoke was a fat, round, brass bowl with a rim, and each was full of milk.

He came down the long veranda crab-fashion, and Premi got up and opened the screen door for him and he went on into the kitchen. The cook gave him a loud *salaam* and brought a cup to measure the milk, which was poured into a big, clean rice cauldron. Then the milk would be boiled and set to cool for the smallest girls to drink in the afternoon.

They counted the cupfuls together, the cook and the milkman, and not another word was said until the two brass bowls were empty. "One," said the cook and the milkman said, "One," and the cupful splashed into the rice pot. "Two," said the cook, and "Two," said the milkman, one after the other to the end.

After the milkman had gone, Chaman came with a garden basket on his head. Whatever was in it would be good, Premi knew, because this was the growing season. Vegetables were larger and flowers more beautiful than at any other time of the year.

She opened the screen door for him, too, and he went inside the kitchen and set the basket down carefully. But when the cook saw what he had brought, she began screaming at the boy. She was so angry that her words ran together and Premi could not tell what was said. She got up and stood with her face pressed against the screen. Some of the other children came running when they heard the loud words.

Missa appeared and Mamma-ji came from the storeroom. The cook paid no attention to her audience. Chaman stood with the basket at his feet, just looking at her and taking the scolding. He was lazy, the cook said. He was late with the vegetables, and she had only one pair of hands to get them ready. She flung them out for all to see only two hands. And the girls were no help on Saturdays. They were doing their hair to look fine on Sunday. And in addition to the boy's lateness, he had brought the wrong thing first. Who wanted lettuces at this time of day? On and on.

Then Missa said quietly, "Let me hear the matter. I will say who is wrong and who is lazy. Let the boy speak."

The cook heard and dropped her two hands and was silent. But even then Chaman did not say anything until Missa asked him to. He pointed to the basket. "This woman is angry, Missa, because I have not brought more."

"And why is there not more?"

"I am alone in the garden this morning, Missa. I could not carry all at one time. She should know that. I did not say I would not bring more. These lettuces here are ready for the shredding, with the good salt and onion."

"But why are you alone? Where is the gardener?"

"The man who looks after the oxen is sick. So the gardener had to take the white ox to the bazaar. It has a loose shoe."

Missa looked at the great basket, piled high with the crisp, curled green of the lettuce heads. She tried to push it with her foot, but it did not move. It was

Saturday in the Yard

heavy, almost too heavy for anyone to try to carry.

She turned to the cook. "Go back to your work, and guard your rough tongue. I will arrange this."

There were more children pressing against the screen now, listening. Bittu came flying across the yard and Lila with her. Their heads were shining clean. Lila said, "What are all of you doing by the kitchen?"

Missa was talking to Chaman, and the children said, "Shh!" They wanted to hear what she said.

"What is ready in the garden, Chaman? What can be brought quickly, if I get you some help?"

"There are tomatoes, Missa, and little potatoes and purple eggplant, ripe for the picking."

The cook said, "Some of each for the curry, though it will be late enough."

"Second class is here," said Missa, "and with small baskets they can bring what is needed, if Mamma-ji will find them the baskets."

The baskets were no problem. Mamma-ji had them in the storeroom. She said, "Come."

Premi forgot about her hair and waiting for Shanti. It would be fun helping Chaman in the garden. She went with the others as she was, without her head scarf, out through the storeroom door and into the vegetable garden in the warm sunlight. Bittu was just behind her and she said, "Now you can talk to Chaman and tell him about the plan. You'll have no better time."

There was only time to nod and press Bittu's hand

before they reached the pile of baskets at the door. Mamma-ji warned them to do as Chaman said and to be careful with the plants.

Chaman decided they could gather the eggplant. It would not take many to fill their small baskets and they would not be heavy to carry. He himself would dig the little potatoes. That was not girls' work. And there were some fat green worms on the tomatoes. He did not think they would like touching those. He grinned at the faces they made.

Some of the eggplant stalks were higher than the children. The long, slender, ripe vegetables were purple and smooth and looked beautiful in the baskets, but their leaves were rough and prickly.

Kamla, with her usual eye out for everyone, said to Premi and Bittu, "Your bracelets will be scratched working here. Better take them off. You should have listened to me. You'll have to mark them yet."

She was right. Premi set her basket down on the ground. She folded her thumb in flat and slid the bracelet off, slowly and unwillingly. Then she wondered what she should do with it.

Bittu was in the next row. She said, "See, Premi, I'm tying mine in my scarf. Oh, you didn't wear yours! Here, let me tie your bracelet up, too."

But Premi said, "No, they'll get mixed up if they are in the same scarf and I want my very own one always, Bittu, that has been mine from the first."

"I can't see that it makes any difference," said Lila, from the row on the other side of Premi. "But hand it to me. I'll tie it in mine for you."

That was better. The picking went on then in fair order and they were almost through when Lila, looking down at her feet, started screaming, "*Sanp! Sanp!*" She threw her basket at a snake coiled in the dust at the foot of the tall plant and almost the color of the leaves.

The others didn't wait to see where the snake was. They followed her, all yelling. Spilled vegetables were strewn after them the whole way to the storeroom door. Kamla fell down and crawled on her hands and knees because she was too scared to get up.

Mamma-ji heard the cries and came running out to see what had happened. "A snake, Mamma-ji!" they said. "Lila saw it!"

But when Mamma-ji saw that they were safe and not bitten, she looked at the trail of purple eggplant and shook her head. What a morning! And Missa had gone away to the bazaar on her cloth-buying trip, so they would have to straighten this out themselves.

The children gathered round her and watched the men beating the garden. They found the snake when it began to seem they wouldn't, and there was a shout when the watchman lifted the dead thing looped over his stout stick.

Then Premi remembered her bracelet and asked Lila for it and they discovered that it was gone. Lila still wore the scarf, but it had slipped off her hair and hung around her neck. And the end where she had tied the heavy bangle was loose and flapping. She couldn't remember anything after seeing the snake.

Premi stood looking at Lila and the scarf but not talking.

Lila said, "I tied it tight, I know I did, but you'd have been scared too, Premi Singh, if you had looked down and seen a big snake. I might have stepped on it."

"Bittu ran too," said Kamla, "and her knot didn't come untied. I should have attended to it, or Premi. It was her bracelet."

Premi said, "It doesn't matter. I'll go back and look. It must be under the leaves somewhere."

"And I will look," said Bittu.

"But first you will all pick up eggplant," said Mamma-ji. "We will need a meal tonight long after that bracelet is found."

She was not joking. She did not smile. So they went back to the garden slowly and stepped cautiously there until their interrupted work was finished. Then Premi and Bittu stayed and Chaman helped them look carefully, everywhere, for the lost bracelet. They went along the row where Lila had been working and on those on either side of it, pushing low leaves aside and watching every foot of ground for fear the snake's mate might be hiding near. But they found nothing among the eggplants.

The sun climbed directly overhead and it was noon before Chaman saw the bracelet, caught on the top of a rosebush in the border round the onion bed. It had evidently been tossed clear of the vegetable garden when Lila's knot had loosened and spilled it out.

Premi couldn't speak for a moment. She had been frightened at the last, believing that it was gone and would never be found. There was a lump in her throat. But she gave Chaman her best *salaam* and held out her hand to Bittu. Once more Bittu slid the bracelet on her arm while Chaman watched.

They were turning away, with all the excitement finished, when Bittu said, "Did you tell him?"

Premi hadn't. When had there been time? But Chaman had heard the question and he waited.

"It's something for Missa, Chaman. For Christmas. We'll have a fair, like market day in the village, and we want all Missa's friends to come and bring things to sell. With the money we will buy her a bell. She wants one very much, a bell for the school tower."

Chaman smiled. His face looked like the sun coming up in the morning, Premi thought. He *salaamed* many times, and he said, "That is a good thing, a present for Missa. My family will give to your market. They are glad I work in this place."

The marking of the bracelets took place that afternoon. All of second class had a hand in it. Mamma-ji's crochet hook and the point of one of Teacher-ji's long *sari* pins were tried. But the nail that the carpenter gave them was the best tool. The initials it scratched were crooked and too large, but Kamla approved and the owners were satisfied.

9

Kamla's Question

One of the greatest problems for second class had been how to get the kite paper. They couldn't ask Missa to send to the bazaar for it. The privilege of buying things was not often denied if they had enough coins, but Missa did like to know the reason, particularly when it was something unusual. Why would girls be wanting kite paper? She would be sure to ask that.

And then Shanti unexpectedly made up for

her earlier coldness by helping them. She wrote a discreet note to their brother in the boys' school and the milkman brought the answer in the shape of a bundle of bright-colored paper two days later. But he gave the bundle to Mamma-ji for them, because he was late and came after school had started.

So Mamma-ji had to be told if they hoped to get any kites made. The bell part was easy to understand, she said, and that they wanted to do something for Missa. But Mamma-ji insisted, as the other grown-ups had, that Missa would like everything much better if she could know about the fair.

Only Chaman had not argued about telling Missa. But he wasn't quite grown up, even though he was doing a man's work in the garden.

Mamma-ji let them have the paper finally, and they went away to begin work on it and review again the whole question of surprising Missa. They still wanted the fair to be a real surprise for her and it would not be if it had to be talked over with her beforehand. She was the one person on the whole compound who hadn't been meant to know from the beginning.

And then the time narrowed and in two days it would be Saturday and the fair would start. How could they wait? Everything was arranged. Every single thing they could do ahead of time was done. The last of the kites were spread out drying on their beds.

The garlands could not be made until the morning

of the fair because the flowers would wilt. But Chaman had promised baskets full of blossoms and Mamma-ji was giving the stout thread and the needles to make the long chains. "We will make all sizes for big people and big girls and little girls," they said. And the price would be pure profit because the flowers were a part of Charity Abide.

On Friday afternoon second class gathered under their teakwood tree. No one had planned a meeting. They were putting in the time of waiting together. It was easier. Premi took the worn paper with the list out of her pocket and read it aloud again.

"We must make one garland specially for Missa," she said. "It will be to honor her from the whole school. When they see her wearing it, the big girls will be ashamed they did not help us. But she will not know. And the bell... "

That was when Kamla asked a question that spoiled everything. One minute they had been sitting quietly listening to Premi talk, with a peaceful feeling that all they had to do now was wait and after sleep, tomorrow would come.

But Kamla said, "How will the school be allowed to come to the fair unless Missa knows we are going to have one? How will all see her wear a garland? Even on big visiting days she never lets us come out on the lawn all at once. And if many people come, she will be too busy to think of us. And there are the Saturday duties. What do you plan to do about those, Premi?"

It was the worst problem they had yet had. Why hadn't someone thought of it sooner? What Kamla said was true. Saturday was Saturday, even if there was to be a fair. There was hair washing and counting the clothes for the laundry and everything else that came at the end of the week. A fair was only something extra. And there was no one but Missa to say how the day could be arranged so that everyone could come to it.

Premi looked round the circle and saw only long faces. No one had any answer for Kamla, who added another point. "The babies will howl if they can't come out. They have folded dozens of pinwheels and windmills and stuck their fingers on the pins. They will want to see them sold."

Then there was silence again. Premi looked at Bittu and Bittu returned the look squarely without smiling and she said, "You'll have to tell Missa, Premi. There's no other way. But she will surely not stop it now when everything is arranged. The surprise will be spoiled, but the whole school will be angry if they don't see our fair. And some have pocket money and will buy if they come."

Premi sat on and stared at her feet. Bittu was right. Kamla was right. Perhaps all the grown-ups had been, as well, and she should have told Missa long ago. The big girls would forget they had laughed at the idea in the beginning. They would want to see what was going on outside as much as anyone. And, because it had been her idea, the whole school would blame her if they had missed any fun.

She stood up slowly. She held out her hand to Bittu. "Will you come with me?"

They left the others sitting under the tree and started for Missa's office. Neither said a word all the way. But Premi's hand was cold in Bittu's warm one. What would Missa say?

It was hard at first to make her understand why they had come to see her when they had got inside the office. She looked at them and thought they were sick. Bittu said they were not and let Premi begin the explanation.

"Missa, tomorrow we are having a fair. We want you to come."

"What kind of fair, Premi? I'm going to be pretty busy tomorrow."

They looked at each other. It was hoped that Missa *would* be busy but not in the ways she was probably thinking about now.

"We planned for an all-day one. It's to sell things like in a village market. To buy you the bell."

Missa said, "To buy me a... What do you mean, child?" She had been writing something at her desk, and she turned away from it and held out both hands and drew them closer so they stood against her knee.

"Now then, that's better. Let's start over again. You are not sick, though you both look it, and there's going to be a fair tomorrow. And you said something about a bell. Sort of a Christmas present for me?"

Premi nodded and Bittu helped. She said, "Yes, Missa, to put in the tower to ring, so everybody can hear. The way you want it. Then we won't have an old gong any more."

Missa's mouth opened and closed and opened again, but no sound came for a moment. Then she said, "But my dears... I had no idea. I thought you meant one of those brass elephant bells they have in the bazaar nowadays... I'd like one of those, too. And have you any idea what a big bell costs? That's why we haven't one. What have you got to sell at your fair? And who will come?"

Premi waved her arm vaguely in a half circle. "Lots of people will come. Many know. We've told our fathers and mothers..."

"And the whole school wants to come out for it, Missa. We are here for the permission."

"So you wait until the night before to ask?" Missa laughed. "You will need the whole school, I think. Not many village people will come in at this time of year, and especially not tomorrow when it's a Saturday between visiting days."

She wasn't cross at all, Premi thought. Just surprised. It was nice that she was, a little. The plan was not completely spoiled after all.

Missa said, "Where is this fair to be?"

"On the visitors' lawn, Missa."

"That is the best place, of course." She looked at

them, not saying anything more for a moment, and they shuffled their feet on the matting and wondered what she was thinking.

Then she said, "Tell the girls they can take turns coming out tomorrow by classes. I will speak to the teachers."

"Oh, thank you, Missa."

They started for the door, but she called them back and they waited while she sat there, poking at her desk blotter with the point of her pen. And spoiling both. But she was thinking, they could see.

"I wish you had told me sooner. I might have helped you get things to sell. Perhaps I can think of something by morning. Never mind. It will be fun, and we can start our holiday that way instead of the picnic I planned for a surprise tomorrow. That's why I was going to be so busy."

"Missa!"

"Surprises all round, h'm? We can have a picnic another day. We will."

They reached the door this time and were going through it before she called them back. She drew them close to her again and she said, "One promise you must give me." They nodded. "It is that you will not be too disappointed tomorrow if you do not make enough at your fair to buy a bell. Your thought is a big, brave one, but sometimes even that kind of thought is not rewarded. Let us hope together that later, after much more thinking and planning, we may have a wonderful bell. I will enjoy the day that you have arranged, and that will be a fine gift for me. Now will you tell the others what I have said?"

"Yes, Missa. Thank you Missa."

The gate was full of children when Premi and Bittu reached it. The news of their errand to the office had got round in no time at all, and the school was ready for news, first hand.

"Is Missa cross?" "What did she say?" "May we come to the fair?"

"All are to come. The whole school," said Premi. "Missa thinks no one else will. But we are to have fun."

The rest of Missa's words were reserved for second class before they went to sleep. And Kamla had the last word again. "Remember what I said. You two can sell your bracelets and nobody need be disappointed. They'd get us a fine bell."

10
Morning of the Fair

The air at Charity Abide was full of the fragrance that dawn brings to gardens. It was a cool smell. There were roses in it and damp earth and a bit of the smoke that charcoal makes before it springs into bright flame beneath the kettle for morning tea. All of it was good.

Many people in Rajahpur and in villages round had waked earlier than usual that morning. It was a day of festival and joy which they had looked forward to for many weeks. The length of it and the joy of it could only be measured by each person for himself. So they made it longer by waking early, as Premi was doing.

She yawned and turned over in her bed. It was Saturday and the first day of holiday. Perhaps Mamma-ji would let them sleep a little longer this morning. And then she sprang up and was not sleepy any more. This wasn't a regular Saturday. Today was the fair! And there were so many things still to be done. The babies' pinwheels and windmills had been collected and stored in Mamma-ji's room. But no one had as yet been appointed to sell them. Or anything else. That was important and they had forgotten it.

But Premi thought of it now while she waited for the gong. She was deciding to wake up Kamla and Bittu and tell them, when she saw, through the arch of the veranda, that Missa was coming into the yard. She was already dressed for the day, and she was walking straight to Middle House without stopping to speak to Mamma-ji.

Some of the others were awake, too, and had seen her. They sat up, wrapped in their warm quilts, and a little low buzz of talk began. Why was Missa stirring so early? She looked a little worried when she stepped into the room, but she smiled at the whispered *salaams* and she said, "You'll have to get up right away. Don't wait for the gong. I need you. The people..." she left spaces between the last words, "I tell you... the people... have started coming... for the fair."

Bittu sat up, rubbing her eyes, and asked, "What shall we do, Missa?"

"Get ready, first thing. And eat something. Then come out and set up your market. The people have come and are cold, and I'm going to give them some tea. They have walked a long way to get here."

She hurried off and they tumbled out of bed. No one in her most excited planning had expected anything like this. Second class had a fair on its hands and it was beginning before breakfast.

They stopped for some warm bread and the glasses of milk that Mamma-ji poured out for them hastily when she heard the news. It was pleasant having breakfast in the kitchen. The brick floor was warm from the heat of the coals over which the big girls were baking the bread. It was more than pleasant also to realize that those big girls were looking at them a little enviously. No one had had much faith in the fair. Now the day was here, and they were the ones to be released from the day's duties. The big girls had to stay inside and bake bread.

Mamma-ji looked them over before she let them go. "Remember that some of the people will be seeing this place and you, too, for the first time today. Keep your scarfs on your heads properly, and be polite." She twitched Kamla's jacket straight. She tugged at Lila's skirt that she thought was too short. She walked with them to the yard gate, and the rising gong began its loud call as they stepped through.

Someone had been at work for them, they found, when they reached the visitors' lawn. Missa? And the men. She couldn't have done it alone. The enclosure had been changed into the semblance of a marketplace. Opening from the arbor, a street had been left in the middle, and on each side of it were spread small cotton rugs, one for each proposed shop. The benches had been shifted, and several set together made a hollow square in a far corner where people could rest.

They counted the little rugs. Ten. Ten shops. The marketplace was ready and they did not have the ten kinds of things to sell. And they hadn't decided who would sell what they did have. But Kamla, who had been the most uncertain from the beginning, was now hopeful. "Things will come," she said. "You'll see."

Missa came hurrying out and heard the discussion about the sellers. "There ought to be two for each shop," she said. "But if Premi planned this fair, she can't stay in one place all the time. And some of you will have to be messengers for me."

They thought Missa still looked worried and wondered why. Everything was going all right, wasn't it? The people had begun to come, hadn't they?

So they portioned out the shops and the sellers sat down, looking very shy and self-conscious and waiting for wares. One rug would be for grain and one for cotton and one for livestock, if any was brought. They hoped for some. It must be as much like a village market as possible. And one for flowers and one for kites and one for the children's paper toys.

At mention of those, one of the sellers got up and left in a hurry, and when she came back, her arms were full of the things the children had made. "The pocket money monitor is giving out the coppers already, and everybody who has any at all is drawing it out. They'll buy when they come out," she reported, and sat down to arrange her shop.

The gardener came with a large basket heaped with some of each kind of vegetable in the garden. It looked like a huge bouquet, the way he had arranged everything in it, and all but the toy seller left their places and crowded round him, admiring the basket and arguing who was to sell vegetables. There were scarlet tomatoes, wiped clean of garden dust, and lettuce, peas, and okra. The potatoes had been washed too, and on top he had spread a bunch of the tiny yellow bananas which grew in the clump by the well.

The early guests to whom Missa had given tea were three women and two men from a distant village. Missa's cook showed them where to sit, and they huddled on the grass in the sun, rubbing their cold hands. After a long, low-voiced conversation, one of the women walked over to the nearest child and offered their gift. It was wheat, tied tightly in a corner of the red and yellow printed head scarf she wore. She poured it out in a rich brown heap, and the seller got up and gave her a deep *salaam*. The market for wheat had opened with this first present from village friends.

When Chaman brought the promised flowers in a wide, shallow basket on his head, Premi was waiting in front of Mamma-ji's room, where a fresh sheet had been spread for the work. The heaps of stemless blossoms made bright patches against it. There were tight rosebuds and some partly open, both pink and red, and quantities of yellow marigolds. But there was not jasmine, the waxy white flowers that made the most fragrant garlands.

"We must have some jasmine, Chaman," said one of the three big girls who had offered at last to help. "You haven't brought any white flowers at all, and jasmine is best."

Chaman picked up his basket and thought a minute, and then he grinned a little. "The Rajah's gardener wanted some American seeds," he said, slowly. "We gave him some. Missa did not know. But we didn't need them. They were left over. And he gave us a new rosebush. If he has any jasmine… " He hesitated again. "Shall I go and ask for some?"

"Oh yes, yes," they said. "Go quickly, Chaman. He will give you heaps. And come back quickly. We need white flowers."

There was nothing more to do here until the

garlands were ready. So Premi went back to ask Missa if she had thought of any other things they could sell. But she never asked the question.

Missa stood on the office veranda, still looking worried, and a man was there talking to her. Five laborers stood at the step under the burden they had carried in on their heads. It was not covered. One could see it was made of dark, polished wood, and parts of it moved when one of the laborers shifted weight.

That was how Premi could tell what the big round thing was. They had had one once in her village at a fair. She had had a ride on it. A Ferris wheel belonged to every fair. This man had brought one to theirs.

"Oh, oh, it's a Ferris wheel, Missa. Say he may stay, please."

"A Ferris wheel?" said Missa, faintly.

"Yes," said the man, "that is it. For the children's fair. Didn't you know?"

"I do now, if I didn't before," said Missa.

"The Doctor Sahib has paid the rent of it and sent me here. The money for the rides is for the fair."

The wheel was not a large one. There were only eight seats, they saw, when it was set up in front of the schoolhouse. The laborers who had carried it in stayed to help turn it. The wooden axles squeaked, but it worked and it was safe, and once it had started it never stopped all day, except to change passengers. That was where a great deal of pocket money disappeared when the classes began coming out. And many watched who were afraid to ride.

Streams of people had begun coming by this time, bringing gifts and asking to see their children. The milkman had done his work well.

The first flower garlands were sold almost before they could be displayed in the shop, because all the parents wanted to get them for Missa. She had eight round her neck at one time, wearing each a little while to please the givers. Bittu had an early turn at messenger service and Premi said, "As soon as she takes them off, bring them back and we'll sell them over again. They're still fresh." Their own special one for Missa would not be needed now. They could sell it, too.

At ten o'clock, when the fair was beginning to overflow to the tennis lawn and the rose garden, Dr. Das arrived with Motibai and his cook.

Motibai had her knitting and she found a shady spot on the benches in the far corner and sat there, seeing everything.

Dr. Das carried a flat, black scratched tin box. He showed it to Missa. Inside there were little sections for coins. "A cash box," he said. "I doubt that the children have thought of a clerk."

"I hope they will need one," said Missa.

"Were you surprised?" he asked.

"Aren't you?" she said, waving her hand about to include all the crowd.

He laughed. "News gets about. They seem happy. I am, to be here. And I think the children may get a surprise or two."

"If you listen, you can hear one of them," said Missa. "A Ferris wheel."

He laughed, gave her a brisk *salaam*, and went off to find a little table. Then he set himself up under the arbor with a cash box open in front of him to hold the collections from the shops.

The cook had brought all the things for a food stall. He had his own little charcoal stove and a bag of fuel for it. He had his pastry board, the shallow, black iron pan for cooking the curry puffs, and all the materials for the dough. The curry he had prepared at home and packed in a tightly covered bowl. All he wanted was a place to work. They gave him a corner where the hedge would protect his stove, and he set up a little kitchen.

The cool smell of the morning was gone now. The day grew warm with the climbing sun and the feet of the people stirred dust. It mingled with the heavy scent of wilting jasmine and of the crowd, and when presently the rich odor of frying pastry floated across the garden and was added to the rest, the reality of the fair was complete. There was little difference, except perhaps the pace and of course the young shopkeepers, from any usual village market scene. In the joy and the color and the noise it was the same.

All kinds of people came, and some that the

children had not invited. Passersby, hearing the sound of the crowd and the squeak of the Ferris wheel, came in and looked around, and went away with windmills and kites for their children.

Premi made the rounds of the shops and her eyes were anxious when she saw the small heaps of coins. They had things to sell but no one was buying.

A huge pile of raw cotton was growing larger and almost hid the small girl who sat waiting to sell some. The wheat of the original gift had been added to many times. There were dried red peppers now among the vegetables. Several chickens and a lone white goose gave Tara, the little livestock seller, plenty to do. The chickens fought until she tied them by the legs so they couldn't reach each other. But when someone brought a loosely woven wicker basket and turned it over the goose to stop it from hissing at people, she complained that no one would buy it if it couldn't be seen.

The goose fell to eating the insects on the grass under the basket and kept moving farther away from the shop. So Tara had to bring it back, when she could leave the chickens.

Chaman's family came a little later, his mother and father and a small brother and sister. They hadn't much to say when he brought them to Missa, but their smiles and deep *salaams* told her a great deal. They were thanking her for giving Chaman work to do.

The mother was holding a black rooster under her scarf, and Chaman showed her where to take it. She set it down by the others, but before she lifted her hands off it or Tara could ask if the legs were tied, a lively rooster fight began. The legs had not been tied. And when they got the cocks separated, the black one escaped to the pile of wheat. It lifted its head in a mighty crow first. The squawking and the chasing drew the crowd that way. Kamla came to help and everybody gave her advice on how to catch the rooster when it left the wheat and flew into the hedge, though her hands had so nearly come together round its bright yellow legs. She was scratched and hot and cross when she finally pulled it out of the bush and helped Tara, the anxious seller, push it under the basket with the goose.

After a while, when the scattered grain had been patted into a smooth pile again, Missa's cook came out and bought all the chickens. He did not want the goose when Tara told him what she had under the basket. Missa had told him to buy chickens. The silver he gave them went into the box on Dr. Das's table. And that was the only big sale of the morning until the goat appeared.

They could hear it coming. The goat seemed to be bringing a man, when they first came in sight. She had brown and white markings and shining hoofs and a proud head. And a nice face, without the mean look of so many goats, though all smelled alike. The man shouted and tried to hold her back. But she had heard the people, and where there were people she had learned there was food, and she and the man had been on the road a long time and she was hungry.

The man pulled on the rope with both hands. But the goat held up her head and said "Baa" at every step and went right on. The man tried to dig his heels into the hard surface of the driveway, but he slid instead, still following the goat, and she was following her nose straight to the marketplace. It led her to an opening in the hedge where the bushes were thin, and then through it, with the man following after and getting scratched. And so they came to the little street.

Food was there, plenty of it, on the ground, where the nanny goat was accustomed to finding it. She leaned and helped herself to a large mouthful of lettuce before the man pulled harder on the rope. Then her head came up again with one torn leaf clinging to her chin.

Children screamed and people came running, and the goat leaped for the pile of wheat just beyond the vegetables. But a basket was there in front of her where no basket had been the moment before, and one of her front hoofs plunged through the frail wicker work.

"My goose!" Tara yelled. "It will be killed. Oh, somebody do something."

The goose honked loudly and the basket moved because of its flapping wings and the goat was freed. No one had to rescue the goose. The basket settled back again over it while Tara was still calling, and the goose walked off hissing softly because of its disturbed feeding.

The crowd closed in then and the nanny was stopped dead still and the man who held her could rest at last. He handed the rope to the nearest person and wiped his hot face with the end of his turban. He was a big man, but he was panting.

"That is the strongest goat I ever led," he said. "Where is Missa? And my daughter Premi? I must give them this present for the bell. The head man has sent this goat, in the name of my village. But his bullocks could not be spared from the fields. So I have walked. Nay," he stopped and took another deep breath, "some of the way I ran to this fair."

No one else had brought such a valuable gift, and the crowd opened for him respectfully when he was ready. He grasped the rope firmly, and the nanny, seeing the way clear before her once more, led on. She went through the arbor at an angle because of the table there. And the taut rope grazed one of the old bamboo supports at the corner. The arbor shook wildly, as if a heavy windstorm were passing over, and then it slowly sank at that corner because the bamboo pole had slanted away from the roof and outward. The trailing rose vine covered the entrance, and there was a loud cracking sound from the side where both corner poles were still upright.

But the nanny had got through before the arbor fell, and Dr. Das came out calmly from the curtain of green and directed the men who came running to help. They cleared away the broken pole and the gardener brought a strong new one, and they held the roof up while he set it in place.

A crowd collected to watch the repairs, so Premi and her father met quietly with no one about except Missa and the goat, which said "Baa" frequently and pulled on the rope.

Premi's eyes were shining. "Papa-ji! It's the best gift we've had. It should make us a lot of money for the bell."

Missa said, "Indeed it should. You will take our deep *salaams* to your head man and to all the village for their offering."

He said, "Did they surprise you, Missa-ji? I thought they should let you know. Sometimes if a surprise is too big, it spoils the gift."

Missa looked at Premi and laughed. "They did let me know, and that was right. But even then I did not understand. And I think today they are the ones to have the biggest surprise. I hope you can stay with us and rest a while."

He looked around, sniffed the fair smell, mixed with goat now, and his eye followed the gathering to the pastry shop.

"A little while," he said, "long enough to visit with my children and eat. Then I must return to the village. Coming twice in one season was not in my plan. But I shall be glad to go back alone, this time."

The nanny said "Baa" again, and he was glad to give the rope to the gardener who would fasten her somewhere out of sight and give her something to eat.

It was Motibai who bought the goat. She took a purse from one of her deep pockets. She counted out the notes, three of them, that the Doctor Sahib asked as the price of the animal. Thirty rupees! And some in the crowd watching the sale exclaimed at the amount.

She said, "I have saved my wage, for I had nothing to buy. Now that I want a thing I have the price. Goat's milk is very good. We will use some of it and the rest I will sell. And in time the amount of these notes will come back to me."

Premi had been a little startled to see the sum of all their activity gathered together here, even though her hopes of success were greater, and had been all the time, than anyone else's. But the sun was almost at the noon mark in the sky, and they would have to do a great deal better during the rest of the day if Missa were to have her bell.

11

Afternoon of the Fair

After her father had gone, Premi made a trip round the shops again. The crowd was thicker and noisier. That was all. There was little difference in the sales. And when she went to the arbor, Dr. Jamna Das said there was not yet enough collected for the bell. How much more was needed she did not dare ask, because she knew now that it must be a great deal more.

She remembered how each grown-up had

exclaimed about the cost of a bell. But not one had spoken the amount in rupees. And second class hadn't asked. They had thought more of the surprise. Maybe their surprise would be greater than Missa's, after all.

The doctor's smile was no comfort. Sales were almost at a standstill. The town people had already come. Those who lived in the farther villages would shortly be starting off home. It was almost the middle of the afternoon.

Premi felt a little sick, as if she were beginning a fever. This was not the season for fevers. But her head felt hot and her tongue was dry and her heart raced. There was only one thing left to do. Whether Bittu did or not, she herself would have to offer to sell her bracelet. This plan had been hers. The blame would be hers. The blame would be hers if it were not a success. Too many had said they did not think it would succeed. But there was still her bracelet, if anyone would buy it. But who here was able to pay all that it was supposed to be worth?

Before she could slip it off and ask Doctor-ji, she heard her name called. "Premi. Premi Singh. Missa wants you." The business of the bracelet must wait.

Missa had scarcely been able to leave the veranda all day. People could find her there easily, and everyone wanted to speak to her. And Premi found now that the crowd had begun moving in that direction too, and she was carried along with it. She had to push and make her own way through, and when she reached the veranda she understood.

An elephant was there in the driveway in front of Missa's house, and the crowd had formed in a large circle round it, though keeping a respectful distance. It wore a holiday trapping of purple velvet embroidered in gold, and on its back was a small, carved, wooden seat with a low railing and soft cushions.

Three men had come with the elephant. One was a mahout who took care of it and went with it always wherever it might be sent. One was dressed in Rajah's livery, a long coat of eggplant color, like the elephant's blanket, with pale blue facings and silver braid. And on his tightly wrapped turban of purple tissue he wore the insignia of the Rajah's house, initials twisted together above a glittering silver crest. The third was only a helper and his clothes were quite plain, but his coat was purple too, like the fruit of the eggplant. And he held a canvas bag tied at the neck with a tape from which dangled a thick, purple, wax seal.

What were these men doing here, this grand messenger and the other two? And an elephant! Premi had never stood so close to one before and she looked it all over curiously. It swung its trunk toward the mahout and made a low sound, and some of the people in the crowd exclaimed and jumped back. But not one of the elephant's huge feet moved, and the man answered its complaint and pushed the trunk away with a short stick he carried.

Missa was reading a letter. And she was laughing inside, but it showed only in her eyes when she looked up and saw that Premi had come. She said, "You will like this, child, very much. I think you can read it for yourself. His Highness' secretary has written in quite clear Hindi."

It was a single page, but it took time for Premi to read it because the crowd was watching her and it was hot in the sun. It must be something wonderful indeed to make Missa look so pleased. And when Premi had finished the letter, she had to go back and read some of it again to be sure she herself understood. If she did, she might not have to offer to sell her bracelet. It seemed that way, if the Rajah's gift was large enough. The sick feeling went away. She would wait and see.

"Respected Miss Sahib," the note read. "Only this morning have I come to know that your school is having a fair to get a bell. Why did you not ask your friends to help? You were my honored guests on *Diwali* night, and the new season has indeed begun well for me. Twins have been born in my elephant stable. My wife has a fine baby son. A suit at law has turned out in my favor. For all these things there should be celebration in which my friends must share. I have made the proper offerings in the temple. Now my messenger will give you, with this, a gift for the bell. And I am sending one of my old, safe elephants to give the children rides. I hope it will make the fair pleasant for them.

"I have the honor to be, Madam,
Your most obedient servant,
H.H. Ganga Ram
Rajah, Mura State"

Premi folded the letter. She smiled at Missa, a little uncertainly. What did one do to accept such a wonderful gift?

The man in the plain coat handed the bag he had been holding to the Rajah's messenger, and he passed it on to Missa. Premi heard the muffled clink of coins as the bag went from hand to hand. The bag was heavy. Missa needed both hands to hold it. How could she make a *salaam* now?

Missa said, "Premi, will you thank them, please?"

Premi put her two hands together, palm to palm, and held them up that way, fingertips just under her chin. She spoke slowly, looking at Missa instead of the messenger to be sure her words were the right ones.

She said, "We of Charity Abide... are honored today, by all our friends. The children will enjoy the rides on this elephant. And please thank the Rajah of Mura for his gift. Missa needs the bell."

The grave face of the messenger had changed when she was through. It would not be proper for him to smile, but he was pleased, she could see. And he gave them both a deep *salaam*.

Then Missa said, "*Ai-ye* — come," and the Rajah's

messenger followed her through the arch of the arbor and into the lawn where the fair was going on again, more noisily, because the news of the elephant and the gift was flying from lip to ear and on again by the same means to the farthest edge of the crowd.

The man visited all the shops. But he stopped at the toy seller's and bought a windmill and the last kite. They were for his own little boy, he said.

The yard gate had been crowded all day with children who had already left the fair or those whose turn was coming next. So they knew about the elephant almost as soon as Premi did. And while the messenger was still taking leave, the ayah came panting out to ask about the rides.

Missa looked up at the sun and said, "There will not be time for all," and the messenger explained that they had not been able to get the elephant ready earlier. "But several can ride together," he said. "There may yet be time."

No one counted the number of trips the elephant made along the half circle of Missa's driveway and out at the gate where the old sandstone post with the verse still stood. Then the mahout said *"Chain,"* and it turned there to go along the public road the full length of Charity Abide compound, as far as the other gate by the well, and in, past the rose garden, and back to the veranda again.

There the mahout said *"Baith,"* and the elephant knelt, and the riders got down. Chaman was there to help the next children climb to the cushioned seat.

Afternoon of the Fair

The mahout sat on the elephant's head between the big, flapping ears. When each group of riders was safely perched on its back, the mahout said *"Ma-eel,"* and the elephant surged up again and the little girls shrieked because they were afraid of falling off.

But no one did. And the elephant went plodding round, again and again, while the sun started down the sky and the people began to go home, until the marketplace was empty except for a few stragglers. The sellers stayed, still alert for a possible last sale.

Dr. Das was counting the day's collection at his little table. Motibai had gone to the yard for a visit with Mamma-ji. The cook's fire was out and he was packing his things. His arms ached, he said, from rolling out pastry. "But they liked my cooking. They said it was better than a real fair."

"But ours has been a real fair, Khansama-ji," said Bittu. She was eating the last curry puff.

"Nay, little miss, though you wanted it that way. But there were no quarrels here and no cheating. Your fair could not be like a real one. All have gone away happy."

Then they heard Doctor-ji calling a welcome to someone and the sound of hoofs in the driveway. The fair was almost over. Who could be coming so late?

It was a tall, bearded old man, stepping down from an open carriage. He wore loose white trousers and a long gray coat, buttoned up to his chin, and a black-tasseled red *fez* sat firmly on his white hair. Men of the Muslim faith wore *fezzes*. And Dr. Das was calling him friend and presenting him to Missa and they were seating him on Missa's veranda.

The children went closer and Missa saw and did not send them away.

He was the Chairman of the Municipal Board of Rajahpur, he said, and he had brought a check, a gift from the city, for the bell. Premi and Bittu looked and listened and their hands clasped. They had not thought any day could hold as much kindness as had already been shown on this one. And now here was more.

The old man said, "There are people of many faiths in Rajahpur, but you must know, my dear young lady, that though you be of one and I another and my friend here still a third, we look together for the greater good of all, each in our own way. That is why the city wants to have a part in this matter of a bell for your school. You did not ask for help. We would not have known had the doctor here not said. But you will not deny us a part? You will accept our gift?"

He smoothed his beard and peered at Missa from beneath his great, bushy white eyebrows.

Missa gave him a *salaam* and took the envelope he held out and she said, "I am glad to accept it. You have paid us honor. You may not know that the children themselves arranged this fair. I am glad they did. They will be in this land when you and I are gone. It is for them the bell will ring, and it will have more meaning for them, I think, because they helped put it in the tower where it will be."

Premi heard the words but she was not really

listening. Those bushy eyebrows of the old man fascinated her. He had a trick with them. They went up and down while he talked. She tried to make her own do the same.

Missa took this guest also to see the place where the market had been and he, too, made a purchase before he drove away. He was the last patron. Now all had gone.

The children and Missa and Dr. Jamna Das stood in the arbor entrance and looked at the visitors' lawn. "The gardener is already grumbling," said Missa. "He says it will take a week of hard work to make the gardens and this place right again."

"What does it matter?" said the doctor. He held up the black cash box and the envelope. In his other hand was the canvas bag. "You will have a bell and enjoy it long after a few broken bushes and trampled grass have been tidied up."

"Doctor-ji!" Premi said. "There is enough?"

He smiled at her anxious face and at Bittu standing close beside her, and he shook the bag so that they could hear the coins striking each other inside it. It was a good sound.

"Enough?" he said. "Enough for a whole chime of bells, I think."

Premi raised her hand to straighten her scarf, just to feel her bracelet slide along her arm. It was safe there, and still hers, because now she need not sell it.

12

In the Tower

The fair was over. No one was in the garden. The benches and shops on the visitors' lawn were deserted. All the people had gone. The big wheel had stopped turning, though the owner had not yet taken it away. He and his men were too tired. They had turned it all day long.

In the dormitory yard the children were walking up and down or sitting about in groups waiting for supper. All were talking about the fair. Everyone had a different tale to tell. The way they had felt when they reached the top of the wheel and how the crowd had looked from that height. The up and down heavings of the seat on the elephant's back until each rider had learned to do as the mahout did and move with it. Others tried to look the way the goat had when its foot went through the goose-basket, and they went round saying "Baa" to everybody. They had seen goats before many times, but not one by itself at a school fair.

Tara, the livestock seller, was still excited about the goose. The man with eyebrows that went up and down had seen the basket moving toward the hedge and asked what was under it. And when he saw, he had bought the soft, white, hissing thing and had it put in his carriage, inside the basket, instead of under it. It was a beautiful carriage, too, Tara said, and the harness had silver buckles.

Everyone had had a fine day, and now that it was over the big girls were telling Premi what a good idea it had been to start the holiday that way. Even Shanti said it.

But Premi was still troubled. Didn't anyone care that because they had had the fair, there would one day be a bell in the tower, the kind of bell Missa wanted, a good one, because now there was money enough to buy it? Wasn't there a single one who did?

Yes, there was one. Bittu. And the whole school would like it when the bell began to ring. But now, tonight, all they could think of were the nice things and the funny things and the surprising things that had made the day a success.

They had sold all they had to sell. At the last there had been only the wheat and cotton left, and Missa had bought them for the school. She sent the wheat to Mamma-ji's storeroom to be ground into flour. And the raw cotton, she said, would be cleaned and fluffed and made into some new tufted quilts.

But Premi knew and Missa knew by this time, because she had been told and so had Doctor-ji, that if Chaman hadn't gone to the Rajah's gardener for the jasmine flowers, they wouldn't have had the Rajah's gift. Missa had laughed about the seeds and the rose bush. She knew the ways of gardeners.

And if Doctor-ji hadn't told the Municipal Board about the fair, the old man with the eyebrows wouldn't have come asking to have a part in the bell. They might not have sold the goose, either, if he hadn't come. The rest of the giving and selling had not yielded very much, so Charity Abide would have had to wait longer for its bell. Without the two big gifts they hadn't dreamed of, the fair would have been only another pleasant time for the school to remember.

But there was also one more thing. Premi hadn't thought of it until now. But it was true. Because they planned the fair, the children had at last brought something to Charity Abide. The cup for basketball

In the Tower

in the assembly hall would no longer be the only gift that could be seen. Second class was giving a bell.

Then she wondered if the bell could be seen from below. There were those small windows up high in the tower. Were they big enough? She had to know that.

No one missed her or saw her go out of the yard gate and along the path to the schoolhouse. She didn't even want to take the time to find Bittu to go with her. She must know now. Could the bell be seen through those little windows?

She stood in the path looking up at the tower. But the sunset light was reflected against it and the windows looked like rosy holes. It would be light inside. She pushed the little door open and went up the dusty steps. The ladder was still there on the platform. If she climbed to that higher place where the bell would be hung, she could see for herself if it would show.

It was a tall ladder and the rungs had been set far apart, she found, for the reach of a man's feet. Climbing would not be easy. She pulled herself up on the first rung.

She struggled up onto the second rung and stopped a moment to get her breath. But that second step had taught her how to do it, and presently she was at the top and knew that the moving bell within the framework must surely be seen from outside, because the little windows were level with the great beams.

She looked out and was surprised to see so much

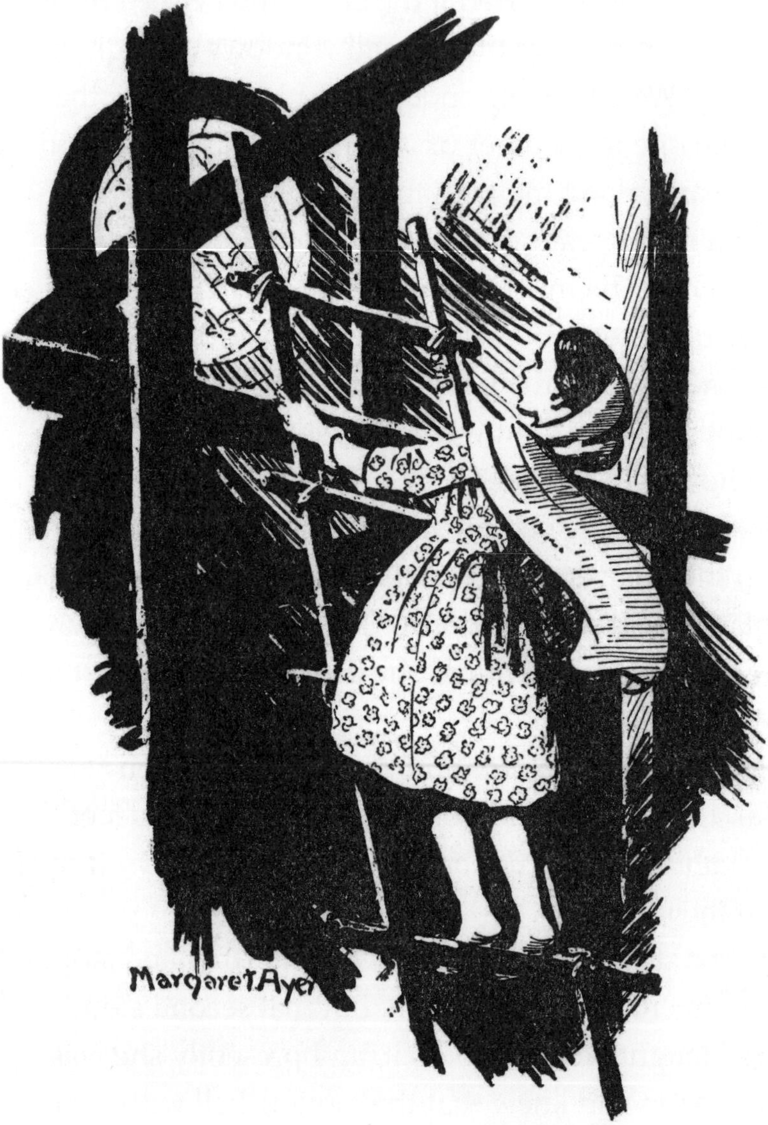
Margaret Ayer

In the Tower

of the town and knew she dared not look down because she had climbed very high. She rested and looked at the thatch and red tile and white plaster of the houses among the trees, under the lovely light of the sunset.

It was quiet up here in the tower and she could think. There had been so much noise all day, all round her, since the early morning. Now she remembered words that had been said, the way people laughed, all the day's friendliness. And the pleasure on Tara's face because she had sold that goose.

That made her think of the old man. She had been too excited to listen when he talked to Missa, but she must have heard because his words were in her mind now. "Though we be of many faiths, we look together for the greater good of all people."

Missa wanted the bell because it was something beautiful that could be shared, and the old man had understood. How many different people had come to Charity Abide today because Missa was seeking something good! An old man and some children and a lot of village people and many from the town. A doctor, a cook, and the Rajah's messenger.

They had come, had had a good time, and had gone away again, but because of that coming together, Missa would have a bell.

The sun was going fast now, and Premi knew she must go while it was still light in the tower. It was even harder getting down the ladder. She could not see where to put her feet and had to feel for each rung. Once the ladder slipped when she leaned too far to one side, and her heart thumped and she rested before going on again more slowly. So it took longer than going up, and when she came out of the little door at the bottom of the steps, she heard the first beat of the mallet striking the copper disk under the kitchen tree. She started to run toward the yard gate. It was suppertime and she was hungry.

The End

Glossary

Ayah [EYE-uh]—an Indian maid or nursemaid

Bundi [BOON-dhi]—a quilted jacket without a collar

Chapatti [chuh-PAW-tee]—an unleavened flatbread made from whole wheat flour and water

Chiragh [CHI-rrog]—a small lamp; from the Sanskrit word "light"

Curry [CURR-ee]—a saucy Indian dish that uses a complex combination of spices or herbs along with meats, vegetables, and/or grains; spices used often include ground turmeric, cumin, coriander, ginger, and fresh or dried chilies

Dahl [dawl]—a dish or preparation of lentils

Diwali [dih-VA-lee]—the Hindu festival of lights, celebrated yearly as a religious holiday throughout India; the name comes from the Sanskrit word *dipavali*, meaning "row of lights"

Fez [fehz]—a flat-topped, conical red hat with a black tassel on top, worn by men in some Muslim countries

Gulab jhaman [GOO-lawb JAW-mun]—an Indian sweet made from milk solids and flour, formed into a small dough ball and deep fried at low heat; the balls

Glossary

are then soaked in a flavored sugar syrup

Ji [jee] — "yes" in Hindi; also a prefix/suffix used at the end of titles or sentences as a sign of respect

Lakshmi [LAWK-shmee] — Hindu goddess of wealth, fortune, and prosperity

Rajah [RAW-juh] — Sanskrit word for king or prince and meaning "monarch" throughout the Indian subcontinent

Sahib [SAW-eeb] — a polite title or form of address

Salaam [suh-LAWM] — a gesture of greeting or respect, with or without a spoken salutation, typically consisting of a low bow of the head and body with the hands or fingers touching the forehead

Sanp [sawnp] — snake

Sari [SAW-ree] — a long piece of fabric that is usually wrapped around the waist, with one end draped over the shoulder, baring the midriff; typically worn with a fitted bodice and petticoat, the sari is considered a cultural icon in India

Tonga [TONE-guh] — a light carriage or curricle pulled by one horse, used for transportation; it has a canopy over the carriage and only two large wheels

Teconas [teh-CONE-uhs] — a fried pastry with three points and stuffed with curry or vegetables, similar to today's samosa

Turban [TURR-buhn] — a man's headdress, consisting of a long length of fabric wound around the head, worn especially by Muslims and Sikhs

More Books from The Good and the Beautiful Library

Mary Ellen
by May Justus

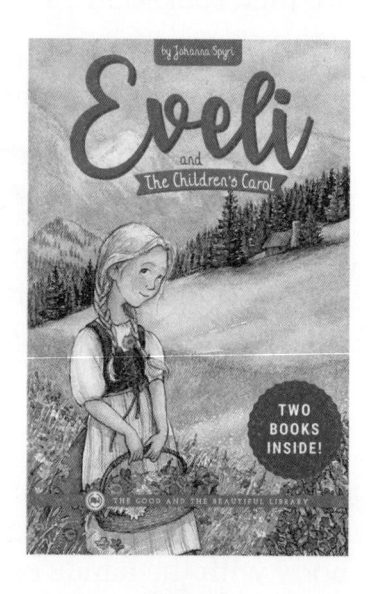

Eveli
by Johanna Spyri

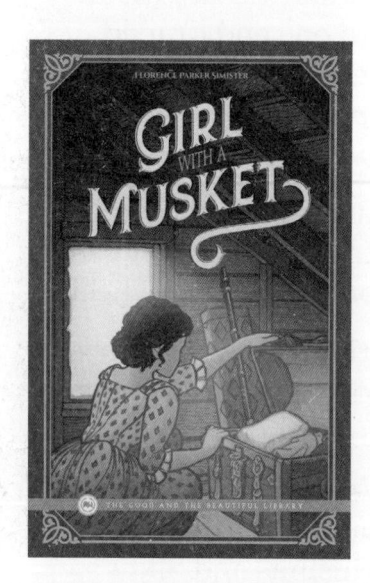

Girl with a Musket
by Florence Parker Simister

Calico
by Ethel Calvert Phillips